HIS CANVAS

Suncoast Society

Tymber Dalton

SIREN SENSATIONS

Siren Publishing, Inc.
www.SirenPublishing.com

A SIREN PUBLISHING BOOK
IMPRINT: Siren Sensations

HIS CANVAS
Copyright © 2015 by Tymber Dalton

ISBN: 978-1-63259-052-7

First Printing: February 2015

Cover design by Harris Channing
All art and logo copyright © 2015 by Siren Publishing, Inc.

ALL RIGHTS RESERVED: This literary work may not be reproduced or transmitted in any form or by any means, including electronic or photographic reproduction, in whole or in part, without express written permission.

All characters and events in this book are fictitious. Any resemblance to actual persons living or dead is strictly coincidental.

Printed in the U.S.A.

PUBLISHER
Siren Publishing, Inc.
www.SirenPublishing.com

DEDICATION

For Sir, because He loves the darkness in the shadows and patiently showed me the beauty there, allowing me to appreciate and grow to love it, too.

And because He's taught me that it's okay to want to spend time there.

AUTHOR'S NOTE

While the books in the Suncoast Society series are standalone works which may be read independently of each other, the recommended reading order to avoid spoilers is as follows:

1. *Safe Harbor*
2. *Cardinal's Rule*
3. *Domme by Default*
4. *The Reluctant Dom*
5. *The Denim Dom*
6. *Pinch Me*
7. *Broken Toy*
8. *A Clean Sweep*
9. *A Roll of the Dice*
10. *His Canvas*

Some of the minor characters who appear in this book also appear in or are featured in other books in the Suncoast Society series. All titles are available from Siren-BookStrand.

This fictional novel depicts scenes of bondage suspension, as well as edge play, utilizing techniques such as cutting and piercings. No play of that type should ever be engaged in by someone without receiving the proper training first and having safety precautions in place. Play safely, peeps. The experts make it look easy only because they've had lots of practice and training.

HIS CANVAS

Suncoast Society

TYMBER DALTON
Copyright © 2015

Chapter One

I love my job.

Askel Hansen peered through the viewfinder at his latest model. She had gorgeous curves in all the right places, distinct lines, beautiful perfection. She wasn't exactly his thing, but as a photographer, he could appreciate her appeal to others.

This shoot was for a regular paying client. They relied almost exclusively on him for their catalog images, meaning a day shooting on location in a gorgeous—if not sweltering—setting south of Crystal River, Florida.

It also meant excellent pay. When he finally returned to Sarasota later that evening, he knew he'd have a sizable check in his pocket without a hint of griping about his rates in the process. Not that he wished all his paying jobs were like this, because that would eventually get boring.

But he definitely didn't mind doing these several times a year.

He straightened and tweaked the position of one of the light bouncers before he took his next round of shots. He'd been at it for a couple of hours already.

Mike Foster, head of the company he was shooting for today, walked down and stood on the dock, off to the side. "How's it going, Kel?" he called out.

"She's a beaut. I think you have a winner with this one."

"Damn sure hope so. Put enough money into R&D on her."

Kel walked over and made a slight adjustment to one of the ropes, which had shifted slightly with her movement, before taking another burst of pictures.

He'd already finished the close-ups, taking care of those inside before they'd moved her out to the docks for the full-on shots. It was fun exploring her many recesses, her tight, enclosed places.

It was a damn gorgeous boat. No doubt about it.

When Kel finally finished the photo shoot, Mike joined him on the dock where his company's latest model sat slowly bobbing on the incoming tide. "Hey, I'm taking the wife and kids out on it in a little while. Going to run out the channel to the head marker and back, then go for dinner later. Want to join us?"

Mike's two kids were adorable. Not that Kel had any desire for any of his own in the near future, but he'd also been photographing Mike's kids in the ten years he'd been doing shoots for Mike's company, Aqua-Knotics Industries. They had a small R&D facility just south of Crystal River, with their main production facility over on the east coast, near Ft. Lauderdale.

He'd originally met Mike and Julie Foster socially several years earlier. Kel had even been the one to jokingly suggest the name of Mike's company when the boat designer quit his job with another manufacturer and went off on his own.

Hell, they both loved shibari. Mike couldn't resist the chance to sneakily hide a clue about his kinky side out in the wide open, in both the company's name and logo. When they had first met at Venture, a private BDSM club in Sarasota, Kel had been honing his rigging skills and his artistic photography techniques. Mike and Julie had lived in Sarasota before striking out with their new boat-building venture.

Mike strongly believed in the old chestnut of rising tides lifting all boats. Literally. He'd hired Kel as their photographer from the start based on their friendship.

Kel surely wasn't complaining.

"I'd love to," he told Mike. "Let me get my stuff packed."

"Awesome. The kids'll be happy to hear that. So will Julie." He glanced around to make sure no one was close enough to hear. "So, how are things going with you? I heard from Mac and Sully it was a little rough there for a while."

"I'm okay. But the next time you hear of me getting involved with someone who doesn't have their shit together, please remind me that it's not my circus and not my monkeys. Deal?"

Mike grinned and slapped him on the shoulder. "Deal." His smile faded. "Sort of hoped she'd be the one for you."

"Well, I did there, too, for a while. Until her crazy started showing."

"Yeah, that's never a good thing."

* * * *

It was nearly ten that night by the time they finished dinner. Kel started his long trek home to Sarasota stuffed from an excellent seafood dinner and his voice slightly hoarse from hours of conversation, both having to shout to be heard while on the boat, and then lots of talking with his friends over their meal.

It was more than enough social interaction to sate him for weeks. Or longer.

It wasn't that he was an introvert, or antisocial, or shy, or any of that. He just didn't have any pressing need for company. He was fine living and—mostly—working alone. Other than his actual photo shoots, the bulk of his work was done at his apartment in the warehouse unit that backed up to Venture. Technically, he probably wasn't supposed to be living there, but since he owned the warehouse complex, no one had complained about it.

He also liked not having neighbors on most weeknights.

Driving allowed him to let his mind wander. Ten years ago, he never would have imagined that thirty-two-year-old him would be a successful photographer and real estate investor.

I hope Dad wouldn't mind.

His mother had never outright asked him exactly why his best friend, Derrick, leased warehouse space in the same building Kel occupied, despite the other man being an accountant.

It would be difficult for Kel to explain to her that Venture was a private members-only BDSM club. Kind of a kinky community center.

One he spent a lot of time at, both socially and for business purposes, having free run of the space during off hours for photo shoots.

Yeah, Mom? I like to tie girls up and do other things to them. And I sometimes even make a little extra money photographing them that way. So does Derrick. So he opened a club because we were running out of party space.

Uh-huh. Suuure. He could see that conversation going well.

Not.

He didn't even mind being single. He'd taken a risk on a relationship that had, as Mike noted, ended in a spectacular blaze of twatwafflery. At least Derrick had banned the girl from the club. Because of her antics, and her batcrap crazy ways, she'd also gotten herself banned from clubs in Pinellas, and even in Orlando.

That takes a special kind of nutjob, right there.

No, he was done with relationships for a while. He wasn't so desperate to get laid that he'd sleep with anyone willing to open her legs. His hand hadn't failed him yet. And as far as play partners, he usually had a full dance card every weekend when he walked over to the club. He'd been single for over a year before taking a chance on the crazy ex, and he didn't have a problem being single again for the foreseeable future.

It was more than worth the peace and quiet in his life.

* * * *

When he returned home, he quickly unloaded everything from his truck into the large bay before wearily climbing the stairs up to the apartment that comprised the second floor of the warehouse space. A previous tenant had, legally and with proper permits, constructed an office up there, utilizing the lower level as their warehouse for their Internet business. It had taken very little for him to add showers to the upstairs bathrooms. He now had two bedrooms and a great room area that was open to the kitchen. He used the office on the lower floor for most of his work, and the large bay area for storage and shoots.

Bonus, the whole thing was tax deductible. He just didn't tell the county he lived there.

The spare bedroom he kept for when models or riggers traveled from out of town and needed a place to crash after a day or night of shooting. He couldn't make a living with fetish shoots, but they helped break up the monotony and he enjoyed them.

After a shower, he made himself a mug of chamomile tea and settled in front of his living room TV with his personal laptop to check his e-mail. Without any shoots scheduled for tomorrow, he could stay up late and then get up whenever he wanted to do all the photo processing for today's shoot.

No, he wasn't what he'd consider rich, even though his bills were all paid and he had some money in the bank. He'd taken part of the insurance settlement he and his mom had received from his father's death at the hands of a drunk driver and wisely invested it with the advice of some of his friends. So far, the investments were slowly paying off. He was looking forward to having a comfortable future when he retired, not trying to get rich quick.

But his vanilla jobs, like today, paid all the bills, with some leftover on the side.

The kinky shoots were gravy he invested back into rigging gear and other supplies. In fact, he'd be doing a shoot this weekend at the club, a series of instructional rigging photos for a friend of his who was writing a book about shibari.

Meanwhile, Kel was building his personal repertoire of skills. He'd been doing piercing and needle play for a while, but had recently started learning branding and cell popping techniques. Not even from a sadistic standpoint, because he really didn't label himself a sadist. But from the artistic point of view, using a model's flesh as a canvas on which to create his art.

It was fun. And it had become a passion in a way he'd never dreamed when he'd first discovered there were people who enjoyed receiving the kinds of things he enjoyed doing to them. As an added bonus, he got to photograph his efforts, saving them, allowing him to savor them repeatedly simply by looking back over the pictures.

Setting his own schedule while making a decent living doing things he enjoyed?

He sipped his tea. *I love my life.*

Chapter Two

I hate my life.

Mallory sat in her car and stared at her phone, at the text message from her uncle, Saul.

Did you complete the application to the master's program yet?

His scathing, piercing tone seeped through the text on the iPhone's screen. She swiped the message and deleted it.

He'd likely be bitching at her about other things by the time she got home that night anyway, so what was one more bitchable offense like not responding to his text message?

No, she hadn't completed the application. She hadn't even looked at the application. She didn't *want* to apply, and was not *going* to apply, either. It didn't seem to matter how many times she'd told him that over the past year, it was like he started hearing the Charlie Brown teacher's *wah-wah* voice coming from her mouth when she answered him.

No. I am. Not. Applying. To the. Fucking. Master's. Program.

Doucheball.

Although she had not as of yet come up with the metaphorical chodes to call him that out loud and to his face. Or in text.

Yet.

Although she suspected that day would soon come if he didn't get off her farking case about it.

I wish he hadn't divorced Aunt Susan.

At least her aunt had been a little bit of a buffer between her and her bristly uncle. But for the past six years, Mallory had been stuck under the same roof as the man.

Miserable.

I wish I'd left with her.

Although, at the time, she'd been sixteen, a minor, and since her uncle was her legal guardian, it would have been too much of a fight to go through it. Better to give in and just suck it up. Although when she turned eighteen two years later, she'd given serious thought about doing it. Except by then her aunt had moved out of state, and Mallory had already been accepted to the Ringling College of Art and Design. Mallory didn't want to go to school anywhere else, especially since three of her friends were going there.

And she had a hard enough time making friends. The last thing she wanted to do was move away from the few she had.

She reached over and cranked up the car's AC another couple of notches. It was a scorching late-April afternoon, meaning May, June, July, and August would be like living in a sauna.

Then again, it beat living up north in the winter. Even though it was difficult for her to remember what South Dakota winters had felt like. She remembered biting cold, and snow, and fun things like going out snowmobiling with her mom and dad, but it'd been so long…

With a shake of her head, she drove away those memories. It only made her cry lately when she thought about her parents not being around to see her academic achievements.

I'm a dang wuss.

She needed to pull her act together before her shift at the consignment store that afternoon. Otherwise, nosy Lucy Scarborough would be all up in her face wanting to see what juicy tidbits she could squeeze out of her and then gossip about to the other employees.

Vulture.

At least it was Friday, and she had this weekend off. The main reason Mallory worked at the consignment store was to get the discount on clothes, when they got any in that fit her. That, and to earn spending money. Considering trying to pry money out of Uncle Scrooge for extras like clothes was nearly impossible, she needed the job despite him riding her about the master's program. He was a tenured professor of literature at New College, with a virtual alphabet of degrees after his name.

Maybe he doesn't understand not all of us want to be academics.

She didn't want to attend USF in Tampa and get her master's. She wanted to finish her final two semesters at Ringling and go to work. She'd already applied to a couple of firms for a summer internship, but hadn't received any responses yet. That had only been a week ago, so she hadn't given up hope. If one of them accepted her, she'd have to get by on the bare minimum weekly stipend her uncle doled out to her without her job at the consignment shop, but it'd be worth it to have her foot in the door after graduation.

I'm going to be twenty-three in a few months. I need to get out on my own sooner rather than later.

She also knew it'd mean finally pinning her uncle down, possibly having to get a lawyer of her own, to unravel the trusteeship her parents had left behind at their deaths when she was ten. She didn't know all the details about it. She didn't even know if there was any money left. For all she knew, there might not be. Every time she'd asked her uncle about it, he'd blown her off and told her to focus on school and then usually found an excuse to immediately leave the room.

At least it was one way to get him off her case about applying to grad school when he hounded her about it.

* * * *

Mallory arrived twenty minutes early for her shift. Much to her relief, Lucy wasn't there.

Even more to her relief, the store's owner, Karen, told her Lucy had called in sick. "Do you mind working late tonight and doing the closing with me?"

On Friday nights, they stayed open until ten. Being close to Ringling, many of the students who got paid on Fridays came in to sell, trade, and buy clothes for weekend parties they were attending. It was their busiest night of the week. And with three large, popular restaurants right around them, they also received a lot of walk-in traffic from patrons.

"Not at all. I'll be happy to."

"Thank you! You are a lifesaver."

Mallory quickly texted that news to her uncle before shutting her phone off, shoving it into her purse, and locking them both in a locker in the back. Snowbird season was quickly shambling to a close, meaning summer cutbacks on hours and possibly even staff. Mallory had been lucky the owner liked her, maybe even felt a little bit sorry for her due to her family status, or lack thereof. Mallory had worked for Karen ever since her high school graduation.

If Mallory had a chance to show that bitch Lucy up, she'd take it in a heartbeat.

There was a large pile of sorting to go through in the back, too. New items to get cataloged and put out on the racks. Aimee Stetson, who was maybe a size two, if that, walked in. She worked the morning-to-afternoon shifts.

"Don't bother thinking you'll fit into any of *those*." Aimee's sharp laugh cut through the air. "I already glanced through them to see what was there. Not a damn thing in there nearly big enough for you to slide over your fat a—"

"*Aimee!*"

Mallory and Aimee both jumped at the sound of Karen yelling.

Despite the heat filling Mallory's face over Aimee's all too familiar jab, the anger on her boss' face when Mallory turned made her gulp. Karen stood in the curtained doorway that separated the back area from the showroom.

And she looked *pissed*.

"*Miss* Stetson," Karen said, icicles forming in the air from her tone. "Kindly grab your belongings and join me in my office. *Right* now."

Mallory barely held back her desire to do a victory dance in front of Aimee. The girl, a bestie of Lucy's and two years younger than Mallory, headed for the break room.

Heart pounding, Mallory started sorting and hanging the clothes, getting them ready to take into the showroom once she knew the coast was clear.

Fifteen minutes later, Mallory heard the buzzer for the front door go off, but when she started toward the doorway, Karen walked through the curtain into the back room.

"Don't worry," her boss said. "It was just Aimee leaving." She sadly smiled. "You want to tell me how long that nonsense has been going on?"

Mallory's face heated even more as she shrugged. "It's okay," she said. "I'm used to it." She resisted the urge to tug at her top. Today she wore jeans and a flowing short-sleeved tunic over them that helped hide some of her extra pounds. At five six and approaching one-seventy, she wasn't exactly svelte, and she damn well knew it.

"No, it's *not* okay," Karen insisted. "Do any of the others do that?"

When Mallory didn't answer, Karen nodded. "Lucy does it, too, doesn't she? I know she's best friends with Aimee."

Mallory studied her sandals. Which, while cute, had cost her less than ten dollars. She'd bought them from the beachwear section at a local drugstore.

Karen finally let out a sigh. "I appreciate you not wanting to be a snitch, but I do *not* want someone like her working for me. No telling what other kinds of shenanigans they're pulling when I'm not around. I only want people I can trust working for me. That means I can trust them with their fellow employees, not just my customers or the till. So for the last time, has Lucy been picking on you, too?"

Mallory couldn't look Karen in the eyes. She forced herself to nod.

"I see." Karen let out a sad-sounding sigh. "The only reason I hired her is because her father is a friend of my husband. I don't need little jerks like that working for me. I know I said you'd have this weekend off, but would you mind coming in tomorrow and working from open until two? I've had several people fill out applications over the past few weeks with summer approaching. I'm sure I can find someone next week to hire."

For this, Mallory could look up. She eagerly nodded. "I'd be happy to. Thank you." A chance to get out of the house and away from her uncle on a Saturday, *and* make extra money?

Hell yes.

Karen gently clasped Mallory's hands and squeezed them. "Don't *ever* let me catch you putting up with that kind of nonsense, all right? You're beautiful. And you have talent. You are the kind of person all those jealous little bitches pray they can one day aspire to be. Got me? So don't let them tear you down when you are the better person."

Mallory nodded. "Thanks."

Karen left her alone to finish the day's sorting. Mallory struggled to walk an emotional line between gloating that the two little bitches would no longer be harassing her at work, and the sad fact that she still had her obnoxious uncle to go home to. In fact, things getting better at work made home feel that much more loathsome.

I hate my life.

Chapter Three

When Mallory finally headed home that night, she didn't even bother taking her phone out of her purse and turning it on. She'd be home soon enough to find out what kind of bitching she was in for when she walked through the front door. She swung through McDonald's on the way for a fast meal, even though she knew it was the last thing she needed.

She didn't care. She wanted it, and considering the emotional ups and downs of the day, she felt she'd earned it.

Her uncle didn't disappoint. He glared disapprovingly at the fast food bag in her hand when she walked through the front door.

"Why didn't you return my texts?"

Mallory didn't slow her progress to the kitchen. "I was at work, Uncle Saul. You know that. I texted you that I was working late tonight."

Unfortunately, he got up from the couch and followed her into the kitchen. "That's no excuse. I texted you before you got to work. I know what time you go to work."

"Not having this discussion with you tonight."

"We most certainly are." He grabbed her arm and spun her around.

Something inside her snapped. She looked down at his hand, where his fingers dug into the soft flesh above her elbow. Then, her gaze slowly traveled up to meet his. "If you don't take your hand off me *right* now," she said, not even recognizing the steel in her tone, "I *will* call the cops and have you put in jail."

He released her like she'd tased him. "How *dare* you talk to me like that, young lady!"

"If you don't want our next talk to be through a Plexiglas divider at the county jail with you on the wrong side of it, you *will* leave me alone. I'm not in the mood to deal with your shit tonight." She grabbed her food and headed for her bedroom, her heart pounding in her chest, nearly painfully, in a way she'd never felt before.

Wouldn't that be fucking ironic, if I gave myself a heart attack arguing with him and needed him to call 911 for me?

She slammed and locked her bedroom door behind her, not knowing or caring if he'd followed her down the hallway.

Her best friend, Chelbie, had been pestering her to talk to an attorney. Mallory hadn't wanted to make waves over the years. She'd wanted to get through college and graduate without having to worry about a roof over her head or bills or all of that stuff. Her uncle wasn't much, but he was—literally—all she had. Mallory knew if she didn't have a basic degree that it would make things that much harder for her when it came time to find a career.

She dropped her purse on the bed and sank down onto the mattress, kicking her sandals off before drawing her legs up. She reached for the TV remote and turned it on, bumping the volume up on a cheesy SyFy movie so she wouldn't have to hear her uncle moving around in the house.

Then she unwrapped her chicken sandwich and started working on that, and the fries.

I need to lose weight.

She hated her ample curves. She hated the fact that her mother's whole family was shaped like a bag of Granny Smith apples, while her father's family—including Uncle Saul—was long and willowy.

Well, except for Saul's pot-belly. And that horrible comb-over.

Then again, maybe having hair and being apple-shaped is a good trade-off.

And she had taken after her mother, other than her blue eyes. Even her mousy brown hair, which she dyed a brassy reddish color, had been her mom's.

Of course, nights like this, she'd give anything to have them both back, looking like a bag of apples or not.

She stared around her room as she munched on another French fry. She'd covered every spare inch of the bland, white walls with her own drawings, sketches, paintings, printouts of her computer art and anime—everything. Her uncle had bought the house and moved them there after the divorce. He had also refused to let Mallory paint the room the way she wanted. He'd told her she could go with white or off-white.

If she couldn't paint the walls, she'd cover them. The unintended bonus that she'd never admit to him was that she could change things around to suit her mood.

At least he'd capitulated and let her make curtains to hide the ugly white horizontal blinds in the window. Swirling purple and turquoise fabric, with silver threads shot through it. The simple sewing machine her aunt had given Mallory her first Christmas with them got plenty of use. Mallory would never claim to be a world-class seamstress, but she could follow a pattern and had made plenty of clothes and costumes for herself and for friends.

In high school, she'd been in the drama club, and almost always ended up helping out with the costuming even if she didn't get much stage time. That, and set design.

Still, it felt good to see her name in the program, recognized for her achievements, for once.

After eating, she dug her phone out of her purse and turned it on. Sure enough, there were messages from her uncle from earlier, which she immediately deleted.

And one from Chelbie sent a couple of hours earlier.

How ya doin girlie?

It wasn't too late to text her friend back, so she responded with several, condensing the highlights of the afternoon and evening.

A few minutes later, her phone rang.

"So when are you moving out of there?" Chelbie asked without preamble.

Mallory collapsed back on her bed. "You know the answer to that."

"Is Slimon right there?" That was one of the nicer nicknames Chelbie had for Mallory's uncle.

"I'm home. Locked myself in my room."

"Gotcha." Her tone softened. "Look, let me talk to my mom and dad about this, okay? If nothing else, you can move in here with us for a while. Please? Life's too short to be this miserable. I can't believe that he's not hiding something from you from the way he acts. He didn't give a rat's ass about anything until you turned eighteen, then he was all hot-to-trot to make sure you stayed in college and applied to grad school. Something's hinky."

"I know." And she did. In her gut, she felt it.

Problem was, she didn't know if she had the strength to fight him on it other than slinging the threat at him that she wanted to see all the trust paperwork to shut him up about graduate school. It felt like she'd spent the past thirteen years of her life in one constant battle after another against the man.

All she wanted was a peaceful life of her own where she could do what she wanted, how she wanted, in her own space, without feeling like she was being harshly judged the whole time.

Even her room couldn't truly be a reflection of who she was. Her bookcase in the corner was crammed to overflowing with mostly used books she picked up at thrift shops and the local Goodwill bookstore. She did buy e-books here and there, and read them on her iPad. The only reason she had an iPad was because she'd needed it for some of her college classes.

It seemed the only time her uncle shelled out money without complaint was for anything relating to her schoolwork.

But she wasn't allowed to hang shelves on the walls. That meant her room felt cramped, tiny, on the verge of exploding from everything she had tucked away inside it. Her dragon statue collection was nestled amongst the books, on the very top of the bookcase, covering her dresser and chest of drawers—even on top of her TV. She had even more, carefully packed away in plastic storage tubs in her closet. She rotated them out every couple of months. She owned very few things that had belonged to her parents, other than pictures. A couple of china cabinets that had apparently been heirlooms from her mom's family. They sat out in the dining room and held a few dishes and pieces of ornamental glassware that had also belonged to her mom.

The rest of the house felt more like a museum than a home.

"We still going to Venture tomorrow night, or is your job going to prevent it?"

"I can go." She didn't know if her uncle was listening on the other side of her door or not, so she was careful not to say too much. "I'll meet you there."

"I heard Tony and Kel talking last week that they're filming a bondage shoot tomorrow afternoon as part of the class. Do you think you can make that?"

"I don't know." Mallory loved watching the rope riggers at the club, the artistry in some of their ties. Especially riggers like Kel, who made the most intricate patterns look stupidly easy to tie.

Not that any of them would likely ever want to work with her. Most of the rope bunnies they worked with were either their own partners, or friends, or had model-worthy bodies.

No one would want to suspend a chub like her.

"Probably not. I'll probably just come for the play session."

"Come on," Chelbie said. "If it's money, I'll pay your way. I sold a book cover yesterday. Class and dinner and the play session. I'm paying. I is flush wit' da moolah."

Mallory laughed. Chelbie had always been able to make her smile. "You are, huh?"

"Yeah," her friend said, returning to her normal tone. "BDSM cover for a self-pubber. They wanted a one-off, not a stock cover, so I made a couple hundred dollars on it." Chelbie was a fledgling photographer in her own right, as well as a graphic artist. She'd traded design work with some friends of theirs in exchange to photograph them for stock photos she could use for book covers.

It seemed they had a tightly knit barter network amongst them. Not that Mallory was complaining about that. She'd picked up extra cash here and there sewing, drawing, and designing artwork for websites or projects for their friends.

It would be nice not having to come back to the house to deal with her uncle after work. "Can I change at your place?"

"Duh. You do not even have to ask."

"Your parents are so cool." Mallory tried not to go there, not to envy her friend's parents.

It was hard not to.

"Yeah, well, they have their moments, girlie." Chelbie's tone turned serious again. "Are you really okay? About what happened today?"

"Yeah."

"Don't let those snarky little bitches get you down. Your boss is right. You're beautiful."

Mallory caught sight of herself in the mirror over her dresser, her brassy red hair pulled back into a ponytail that hung down to the middle of her back.

Right now, the last thing she felt was beautiful. "Yeah, well, you're biased."

"Stop it," Chelbie said. "I mean it. Don't brush me off like that. I love you like a sister. You know that. I will never lie to you. I'm not exactly a twig myself."

"Yeah, but you don't need to buy sizes with an X or W tacked onto the number, either."

Chelbie's tone gentled. "Then let's do something about it. Both of us. Let's start walking once a week or something. We can go out to Siesta Key and walk the beach at sunset one evening a week. We've been talking about it. Won't cost us a damn thing except the gas money to drive over there."

Mallory knew she needed to do something. She wasn't happy with herself. It didn't take a rocket scientists to put together the basics. She ate to comfort herself and feel better about her emotional situation. She hadn't even needed the basic psych class she took a couple of years ago in school to tell her that.

"Okay," Mallory said. "We'll talk about it tomorrow. I'll text you after I get off work and I'm heading your way."

"Deal."

Once Mallory got off the phone, she pulled herself to her feet and walked over in front of the mirror.

Mirror, mirror, on the wall. Who's the fattest of them all?

Okay, so that wasn't fair, either. She knew plenty of people, some of them friends, who made her look skinny by comparison.

I don't like myself. *It's not just my body I'm sick of.*

She turned off her cell phone and set it on the dresser after plugging it into the charger.

It'd be easy for her to blame everything that went wrong in her life on the death of her parents. She also knew if she kept doing that, nothing would change.

I'll never change.

She forced herself to stare into the mirror again.

One evening a week. Baby steps.

If she could do that, and keep doing it, she knew she could make it a habit. It was how she'd managed to force herself to study in high school, and now in college, when all she'd wanted to do was drown her sorrows in Publix glazed donuts and mindless TV.

Maybe I should talk to Chelbie's parents.

Shelving that decision for now, she started getting her things ready to go take a shower.

Chapter Four

Mallory didn't bother making a pot of coffee Saturday morning as she prepared to leave for the store. She'd hoped to make her escape before her uncle arose, but no such luck. She sensed his presence in the kitchen doorway without even needing to turn around.

"What are you doing?" he finally asked.

"Getting ready to go to work."

"You don't work today." He walked over to the calendar hanging on the fridge. "You have it marked off here."

Of course he'd look at the damn thing when it suited him. "My boss fired two people yesterday and asked me to work today to fill in."

"I want to talk about your grad school appli—"

She whirled around. "*Stop* it! Just stop it. For the last damn time, I am *not* applying to grad school. I'm getting my four-year degree, and then I'm getting a job. Unlike some people in this house, I'm not content to spend my life sitting in a university office pushing papers around."

"You could make so much more money with a—"

"What the *hell* is *wrong* with you?" she yelled. "Why are you refusing to take 'no' for an answer? And after all, let's face it, the money I'll save not going for an advanced degree is money I can use to move out and get my own place. I'd think you'd be happy about that as much as you harp on me all the time about every damn thing I do wrong around here that's not up to your standards."

One of the few good things she could say about her uncle was that he wasn't a slob. And he did pull his weight around the house with cleaning and other chores. She'd had housekeeping drilled into her head within the first few months she lived with her aunt and uncle.

It was one of the reasons she now refused to make her bed every morning. One small rebellion that gave her a little satisfaction.

"After all I've done for you through the years, young lady, you could show a little gratitude and respect."

"Okay, for starters, the respect you lost a long time ago when you and Aunt Susan divorced." There, she'd said it, and it felt damn good to get it off her chest. "Secondly, yes, I do appreciate that you guys took me in and raised me. I do. Thank you. It's also why I'm doing my damnedest to stand on my own two feet and be independent. Why you're fighting me so hard on this is beyond me."

"You are just like your father," he spat. "Ungrateful, spoiled brat."

"Spoiled? Seriously? I've felt like a stranger in what was supposed to be my home, too, ever since I've been living with you. When we moved here after the divorce, I thought okay, maybe with that behind us things will change for the better. Nope, you've gotten worse. Like you're the caretaker here and I'm an inconvenience."

She stormed out of the kitchen. She'd planned to grab a light, healthy breakfast, some fruit and yogurt from the fridge, but now all she wanted to do was leave. Fortunately, she'd already packed her stuff she'd need for going out to dinner and the club with Chelbie. She grabbed the duffle bag, her purse, and her laptop case off her bed and turned to leave, just to find her uncle standing in the bedroom doorway and blocking her way.

"Move."

"We are going to discuss this, and you are not leaving this house until you agree to apply to graduate school."

There was something…odd about his tone. Borderline desperate, if she was forced to apply a label to it.

It creeped her out.

"I'm twenty-two years old," she said. "Almost twenty-three. I think I'm capable of figuring things out for myself from this point on." She wanted to walk toward the doorway, but he had about six inches on her in height and she wasn't sure if she was strong enough to simply power her way past him.

"You don't know anything about the world. You're just a kid. You need a graduate degree to get ahead in the world."

"No, I need you to get out of my way to get ahead in the world." Time to drop the bomb. "I've already put out applications for internships this summer. And if I'm offered one, I'm taking it because it'll be a foot in the door. I'm already earning money here and there doing freelance design work, in addition to my job. I'm confident in my skills and my four-year degree."

His jaw tightened, muscles working like he was trying to figure out what to say, or maybe he had something to say and couldn't force it out.

Maybe it's early-onset Alzheimer's. There was a history of it in his family. On both parents' sides.

Lucky me.

She didn't even want to think about that right now. That she might feel morally obligated for his care because he'd taken her in when she'd been orphaned.

She didn't blink, meeting his gaze and holding it. She sensed if she backed down at this instant that he would relentlessly hound her about grad school until she finally moved out.

And despite his shortcomings as a person, he was her family.

Her only family.

Part of her couldn't bring herself to forever sever that last connection yet, no matter how flimsy and tenuous it was. To do that meant she was truly alone in the world.

While he might have been a crummy emotional safety net for as long as he'd been in her life, he had kept a roof over her head, food in the fridge, made sure she got to the doctor, and helped ensure she got into the college she'd wanted to attend.

He blinked first, stepping back. She swept past him, adrenaline shakes hitting her as she pulled the bedroom door shut and made a beeline for the front door.

She was aware of him following her.

"We'll discuss this when you get home from work," he said.

"I won't be home until very late, if at all. I'm likely going to spend the night with Chelbie at her house. We're going out with friends tonight. In fact, don't expect me home before late Sunday night."

She slammed the front door behind her on whatever protests he might be offering up about that plan. Not looking back, she raced to her car, tossed her stuff into the passenger seat, and pulled out of the driveway without looking back. Tears rolled down her face as she cried. She tried to blink them away but now that the dam had cracked, the flood wanted to burst free.

And, she belatedly realized, she'd pulled out of the driveway without buckling her seat belt. She realized that when she spotted flashing red and blue lights in her rearview mirror a few minutes later, just seconds after she'd figured out the annoying dinging sound she kept hearing was her car pestering her to buckle up.

Dammit.

The deputy who walked up was an older man. "Ma'am, do you know why I pulled you over?"

She burst into tears. "Because I had a fight with my stupid uncle and forgot to put my seat belt on." At that point, she was beyond caring if he thought she was trying to get out of the ticket or not. She laid her head on the steering wheel and cried, knowing a ticket would blow through whatever she had in the bank and be one more thing her uncle could lord over her head.

"Ma'am, please calm down. I need to see your license, registration, and proof of insurance."

She dug through her purse to find her wallet and tried to hand it over, but he said, "Ma'am, just the license, not your whole wallet."

Her vision blurred through her tears as she fumbled through it and finally pulled it out. She'd never gotten a ticket. Not a speeding ticket, not even a parking ticket. She'd never been pulled over before. Ever.

Rummaging through the glove box, she finally found the envelope with the registration and insurance paperwork and handed it over, too.

"Wait right here for me, ma'am."

She nodded, grabbing a handful of napkins shoved in the center console between the seats and trying to clean herself up. At least she hadn't put makeup on yet.

Raccoon eyes. Just what I'd need on top of everything else.

When he returned a few minutes later, her heart sank when she spotted the clipboard in his hand.

"You have a clean record, so I'm going to do you a favor and give you a warning citation," he said.

"Thank you!" She burst into a fresh round of tears, barely hearing what he said as she signed the warning with trembling hands.

And then she put her seat belt on.

He returned her license and paperwork and she jammed them into her purse, not even bothering to try to return them to their proper locations.

"Ma'am, are you all right?"

She shook her head. "I've got an asshole for an uncle who insists for some damn crazy reason that I have to go to grad school when all I want to do is graduate from Ringling and go to work."

She couldn't read the expression on his face.

"I'm sorry," she quickly added. "It's…complicated."

"Are you being abused?" he asked. "I can get you some information on resources to help you out."

A gurgling snort escaped her. "No. I *wish*. Then I'd get the hell out without a look back."

She didn't know what was worse, having to admit all that to the deputy, or the expression of pity that he wore when she did.

He tore the citation off the pad on his clipboard and handed it through her window. "From now on, make sure you put your seat belt on. And you might want to see if Ringling has any counselors on campus who you can talk to about your home issues. Try to have a good day."

She stared at the slip of paper, her gaze settling on the side view mirror and the deputy's back as he returned to his cruiser.

That's actually a damn good idea.

She'd never really thought about it before. She'd been so used to doing things on her own over the years that seeking assistance from the school had never crossed her mind.

She shoved the citation into her purse with her license and paperwork, double-checked her seat belt was securely fastened, and then pulled back into traffic when it was safe.

Maybe I can develop sudden appendicitis or something. Or trip and fall and break my neck at work. That would make this day absolutely friggin' perfect.

Chapter Five

Mallory got to work and immediately headed to the bathroom to wash her face and put her makeup on. When she emerged, Karen was waiting for her.

"Are you all right?" Karen asked.

The concern on the older woman's face nearly started her crying again, but, somehow, Mallory held it together. "Just a bad morning. Fight with my uncle. Then I got pulled over and issued a warning because I forgot to put on my seat belt."

"How'd you forget to put on your seat belt?"

"Because I had a fight with my uncle."

"Ah. Sorry." She tipped her head toward the office. "You blew in so fast you didn't give me time to tell you I brought caramel lattes for us."

Mallory hugged her. "Thank you! You are the best."

Karen led the way back to her office. "Well, I'm a firm believer in treating people well and rewarding them." She turned to glance at Mallory. "And considering I feel horrible those little bitches were treating you like that, it's the least I can do."

Mallory's face heated. "It's not your fault."

"Why didn't you tell me?" In her office, she rounded her desk and reached for the cardboard carrier holding two cups. She placed it on the desk in front of Mallory before taking one of them herself.

Mallory took the other. "I didn't want to make waves." She shrugged. "I'm used to being picked on because I'm fat."

"You're not fat."

Mallory tipped her head to the side. "No offense, but you need glasses. Seriously."

"Okay, so you're a few pounds overweight. Who isn't?"

Mallory sipped her latte. It was delicious. "I know I need to lose weight. I also know, yeah, I could be a lot bigger than I am. I've been holding steady at this weight for about six months. I've been trying little things, like parking farther out at school and here, things like that. I just haven't had time to try to figure out an exercise routine."

"If you need any help, or want any guidance, let me know. My sister is a doctor. I'm sure she'd slide you in for a consultation. And I have a family membership to the Y. I can always add you on, if you'd like. I know your funds might be tight right now."

Mallory struggled—and finally won—the battle against her tears. How could her day have two diametrically opposed sets of emotions when she'd been awake for less than two hours?

"I really appreciate it. Right now, I just need to get through the next few weeks." She took a deep breath. "I think I need to look at moving out on my own."

"Good for you. I know you haven't been happy there with your uncle."

"Yeah. The problem is, I need to save up for it. I don't know how much money there is in my trust, beyond school funds and stuff. Or if there even is any and he's been paying for it out of his own pocket." Which would make her feel guilty as hell in some ways for how she'd reacted to him, but didn't change the fact that her uncle was still an asshole.

"We can always talk about putting you on full-time here."

Mallory thought about those internship applications floating around in the ether. She didn't want to pin her hopes on any of them and not have them come through. Meanwhile, she needed solid income she could count on.

"Thanks. I'm hoping my uncle calms down by tomorrow and I can sit down with him and discuss things without him blowing up."

"Would you like me to be there with you when you talk to him? Provide a buffer?"

"Actually, that might not be a bad idea. I'll let you know." Mallory took another sip of the comforting latte. "He's just really crazy on this idea about me going to grad school, even though I keep telling him no. I don't get it. I don't have a scholarship for it and doubt I could get one, so the money's either coming from his own pocket or anything left in the trust. You'd think he'd be happy I'm saving him all that and want to earn a living after I graduate."

"Maybe he's just worried about your future. Not that I know him," Karen quickly added, "but maybe that's his dysfunctional way of trying to show you he cares."

Mallory considered that. Saul and Susan never had kids of their own. Mallory never got the full story of why, either. She took a deep breath and slowly let it out. "Maybe you have a point," Mallory conceded. "I keep thinking he's acting like a jerk. Maybe he's got a reason for it."

"Or a reason he thinks is valid. Again, I'm not trying to dismiss your—"

"No, I get it. I hadn't thought about it like that." Mallory hated conflict. Despised it. "Once we both cool down, I'll try talking to him about it again and see if I can't get him to tell me why he's so hyper about me going to grad school."

"That sounds like a very sensible plan."

* * * *

When Kel walked over Venture a little before one Saturday afternoon, he wasn't surprised to find Tony, Shayla, Seth, and Leah already there. Even if they hadn't been there, Kel had a key of his own.

"You need any help with your gear?" Tony asked him.

Kel started unloading the cart off to one side of the large space. "No thanks. Just one more run and I have it all. I didn't feel like loading it all in the truck."

"We need to cut you a door through the back wall," Tony joked. "Save you some time."

Kel smiled. "I don't mind the walk." He knew his friend was kidding, but he valued his privacy far too much to do that. "We doing dinner tonight?"

"As usual," Seth said. "Sigalo's." A group of the close-knit friends frequently ate dinner together on Saturday nights before heading to the club. The roster varied, but a core group of people almost always attended.

Kel grinned. "Hey, Tony. Any more of your employees going to show up?"

Tony rolled his eyes. "Jesus, don't curse me. I'm just glad Mike and his wife have fit in with everyone."

Shayla laughed. "I'm now required to find out the particulars of anyone new who joins our book club," Shayla said.

Mike's wife, Jenny, had become interested in BDSM via the book club. The two women didn't know their husbands worked together.

"I like Jenny and Mike," Leah said. "They're sweet. They're so cute to watch when they play. Newbie kinksters, just learning the ropes."

"Mike has come a long way in his rigging skills over the past few months," Kel said. "Very impressive ropework."

"I'm trying to talk him into learning suspension," Seth said. "I know he could easily do it, but he doesn't think he's got the skills."

Kel unloaded his cart. "Well, better that than he's trying to string people up his second week in the lifestyle."

Everyone snorted and laughed in agreement.

"I'll be right back," Kel said as he towed his empty cart toward the door leading to the lobby.

"Sure you don't want any help?" Tony asked.

"I do this for a living," Kel assured him. "This is an easy job." He headed back around the end of the building to his place. He didn't mind the exercise. He didn't do enough of it normally. While he wasn't fat, he'd put on ten pounds in the past few months that he knew he needed to get off his six-foot frame before it settled in for good.

He didn't know how many people were supposed to be there today for the afternoon class. Well, demo. Not so much a class. Scrye, whose real name was Mark, had invited people to come watch the presentation while Kel shot it. Attendees had to reserve their place for the limited number of spots, but Scrye liked the energy a crowd brought to a space when rigging.

Yeah, a little bit of an ego, but not any worse than most of the riggers out there. In fact, the man was a lot more modest and easy to work with than many of them.

Kel didn't care. He was there to point and shoot the rigging. It wasn't a job that would pay a lot in terms of money, but it would get his name out there more as a photographer and boost his own portfolio. Especially since the model, Scrye's wife, June, had signed releases allowing Kel to monetize some of the shots for resale. He had a couple of book cover artists that frequently purchased images from him for their work.

Scrye blew in twenty minutes later like a miniature tornado, deep belly laughs and mile-wide grins aplenty as he started getting things ready.

Kel often wondered if June was a naturally calm and placid person to put up with such a large and turbulent personality all the time, or medicated just enough so it didn't bother her. Scrye was a great guy, but his energy would overwhelm Kel after too long. Like mainlining caffeine.

At least I don't have to live with him.

* * * *

At one o'clock, one of their other part-timers came in to help, and Karen set Mallory free for the afternoon.

"Go have some fun with your friends. Or talk to your uncle. Or something." She smiled. "I appreciate you coming in this morning to work. We'll talk about the new schedule next week. Enjoy the rest of your weekend."

Going home wasn't on Mallory's agenda. She sat in her car in the parking lot with the engine running and the AC struggling to cool the interior while she texted Chelbie.

You home? I'm done at work earlier than I thought I'd be.

A moment later, the phone rang in her hand.

"Get your butt over here right now."

"Why?"

"The class. Duh. Scrye is rigging at the club this afternoon. He's doing a demo for a photo shoot. I already emailed the club, and they said there were a couple of spaces left. If we leave when you get here, we can make it there before it starts. Street clothes are fine, meaning you don't have to change from your work clothes."

"I can't aff—"

"*Free*, girlie. Drivest thou with haste. Hasta la bye-bye." She ended the call before Mallory could offer up any other excuses.

With a sigh, but feeling a little lighter in spirit, Mallory dropped the phone into the passenger seat, made sure her seat belt was fastened, and headed toward Chelbie's house.

Maybe the day isn't a total loss after all.

Chelbie had a way of taking over and brightening Mallory's mood in a seemingly effortless way. Mallory loved her for it. Mallory had no sooner pulled into Chelbie's driveway than her friend bounded out of the house and impatiently started yanking on the passenger door handle until Mallory hit the unlock button.

After helping Mallory get her stuff moved to the backseat, Chelbie slid into the seat, closed the door, and got her seat belt fastened. "Off, ye lover of lattes! Release the Honda hounds and speed therily to..." She waved at the windshield. "Floor it, sister."

"I've already had one brush with the law today. I don't need another." She shifted it into reverse and carefully backed out of the driveway.

Chelbie dropped the act. "What? What happened?"

Mallory was almost in tears again by the time they reached the club, but she'd gotten the whole story out to her friend.

Chelbie frowned. "Seriously, we need to talk to my parents and get their advice about this."

"I don't want to bother them." Mallory noted the parking lot was half full. "And I don't want to get upset before we go inside." She took a deep breath and fanned her face, leaning in so the cold air from the AC vent blew on her. "Let's get in there before we miss anything."

Chelbie reached across the seat and laid a hand on Mallory's. "You're my best friend, and I love you. You always have a place if you need it." Chelbie's bright, cardinal-red hair was cut in a short pixie style that looked adorable on her. She'd been blessed at birth with light blonde hair that she despised for some unfathomable reason. Today, she'd used dark eyeliner and blue eye shadow, combined with her midnight blue tunic and black leggings with short boots.

She was adorable, where Mallory felt frumpy and loathsome by comparison. Through no fault of Chelbie's, either.

"Don't make me cry. Let's go watch some rope."

Chelbie studied her a moment longer before finally unfastening her seat belt and reaching for the door handle. "I might volunteer you to get tied, you know."

Mallory's face heated. "I don't need to be a rope bunny." She'd been dying to try shibari but had yet to work up the courage to ask one of the riggers to tie her.

Ironically, she'd had no problem asking other Tops, like Landry or Cris, to do impact play on her. She never engaged in sexual play with any of them, and always kept a bra and panties on when playing, but she loved the sensations of impact play.

It was one of the few things that allowed her to escape her brain for a couple of blessedly worry-free moments.

"You need a playday," Chelbie insisted as they got out. "And I'm going to make sure you have one if it kills you." She shut the passenger door and headed toward the lobby entrance.

At the rate my day's going, it just might.

Mallory shut her car door, shouldered her purse, and hit the button on her key fob to lock the car before following her friend.

Chapter Six

Kel got his lights arranged around the club's large metal A-frame suspension rig Scrye would be using for today's demo. They hung a black fabric backdrop on the wall behind it to hide the faux stone paint design on the wall. The focus needed to be on the model and the rigging, not the background.

The audience would be seated in front of the rig, but behind Kel and his cameras. No one would be allowed behind the rig this afternoon, to prevent people from accidentally walking into the shot. Seth and Tony would stand off to either side as spotters, but well out of the scene.

Where Scrye was like a large grizzly hopped up on dark chocolate and triple espressos, June was a slim, petite anchor of white marble with a quantum gravitational pull of calm on the man. A former gymnast, and now a yoga and gymnastics teacher, the forty-year-old woman could still easily contort her body into positions that would put the average nubile coed into traction if they attempted them.

Kel liked shooting their work because of the variety they brought to a scene, but truth be told, he wasn't personally attracted to June. She was pretty, and definitely in shape, but…

There was nothing different or discernible about her at all.

Nothing remarkable.

She could be any one of thousands of nameless bondage models out there.

And because of her work, June absolutely could not take any kind of impact play or other play that might mark her in suspicious ways. The incidental bruise she could easily explain away as an occupational hazard. But Scrye had to be very careful with her in sessions not to let her hang too long, or tie her too tightly, and mark her with ligature bruising.

Which was a shame, because that was exactly the kind of thing Kel enjoyed.

The process as much as the result fascinated him. The pliability of human flesh, the way it responded, rebounded, transformed and then back again after play.

By the time they were ready to start, they had at least thirty people in the audience. Kel stood off to the side and watched Scrye go through his usual spiel, a mix of humor and safety warnings filled with as much energy as the rest of his play.

Kel was beginning to think the man didn't have an off switch.

For the shoot, June would wear a mask across her eyes, a G-string, and a bandeau top that would conceal her breasts without interfering with the rigging. That was both to keep the book from getting slapped with an "adult" label as much as it was for her own privacy. In their personal play at the club, he usually tied her fully naked.

As Kel scanned the audience, he recognized many of the faces. Some of them were good friends, some acquaintances, and some people he'd seen at the club before, but whom he didn't know very well.

One woman in particular caught his eye. He'd seen her, and her friend, at the club dozens of times over the past year or so. He'd also seen her play with a couple of different Tops, but never sexually.

He'd never seen her tied, though.

As he studied her from across the room, her attention safely focused on Scrye and June, Kel's eyes took in her voluptuous curves. He knew some men, whose perfect ideal of a woman meant a single-digit clothing size, might label her fat, but she wasn't ugly by any stretch of the imagination.

He wondered how she'd look tied up, the kinds of ligature marks that would be left embedded in her flesh after releasing her, if she was interested in needle play—

He shifted position when he realized his cock was starting to respond to the mental masturbation he'd subjected himself to. He thought her name was Mary, or Marcia, or something like that, but he'd never talked to her personally.

I'll have to remedy that.

He watched her rapt attention as she watched Scrye. Her long, reddish-orange hair was too bold to be a natural color, but it looked perfect on her, accentuating her blue eyes and bringing out the creamy tones in her skin.

I want my ropes on her.

Whoa. Calm down.

This wasn't like him, to get excited about someone. Hell, he didn't even know if she wanted to be tied up. She might just be there with her friend, or simply curious.

He forced his focus back onto Scrye.

I will *try to talk to her today. At least introduce myself.*

* * * *

When the rigger started his first tie, Mallory risked a glance at the photographer. She was pretty sure his name was Kel, and she'd seen him at the club many times.

Once again, her own fear kept her from speaking up, from introducing herself. He played with slender women. At least, that's all she'd ever seen him play with.

Why would he ever want to play with me?

The best riggers at the club were always busy during play sessions. They usually drew a crowd and had a waiting list of people wanting to be tied by them.

Yes, it was true, she saw a large variety of body types in the lifestyle. People who made her look like Jabba the Hutt, and people who made her look like an anorexic model, and everywhere in between, from ages eighteen to eighty-something.

Still, this was *her* body. And her self-consciousness held her back. In this regard, at least. Playing with other Tops hadn't been an issue. She'd seen people playing with everyone from the skinny to the obese.

Rope riggers, however…

It just seemed that, unless it was their own partner, they rarely tied anyone on the…larger end of the body frame scale.

Of course, she wasn't at the club every night it was open, and this was the only club she attended on a regular basis. Maybe her fellow chub club members got plenty of play on other nights, or at other clubs, or even privately.

That would be my dumb luck, wouldn't it?

Chelbie leaned in and whispered in her ear. "You going to talk to that guy today, or do I need to do it for you?"

"You wouldn't!"

"Watch me. Well, not right now. He's busy. Duh."

Mallory's heart raced. Chelbie was rarely a person of idle threats. If Chelbie thought someone needed a hard, loving shove in the right direction, she was more than happy to give it in any way possible.

Now Mallory desperately tried not to look at the photographer, sure that if he caught her staring at him that he'd think she was some sort of weirdo or something.

Relatively speaking, considering what they were all there to watch.

Normally, she didn't have a problem talking to Tops and asking to play. She'd seen enough of them play, and knew enough of them by talking with others—and the Tops themselves—to feel comfortable approaching them.

The mental block about rope riggers was one she wished she could break through. Get the initial rejection out of the way.

If only she felt she could live up to the high expectations that invisibly hovered around the rope scenes she'd watched, maybe she wouldn't feel like that.

Mallory leaned her head close to Chelbie and whispered, "Isn't there a rope club or something?" She hoped her comment might get her friend to relent and not bug the guy on her behalf, if Chelbie thought she would take the initiative herself.

"Meets every other week, on Wednesdays."

"Oh." That left her out. She usually worked Wednesday nights.

So much for that plan. Maybe if she went to some of the club meetings, she might find a way to get herself over the emotional hump, so to speak.

As they watched Scrye work, Mallory snuck glances at Kel. Now that he was actively photographing the rigger, his focus apparently lay totally on the job at hand. His short brown hair had tousled slightly as he worked, his brown gaze intent. He was around six feet tall, built lanky with lean muscles and long, nimble fingers she supposed knew their job very well, regardless of what he was doing.

He exuded a quiet calm, in direct contradiction to the boisterous rigger the audience raptly watched.

Chelbie poked her in the side and grinned, sending a flush of heat straight to Mallory's face. She recognized that sneaky look her friend wore.

Like it or not, Mallory would end up talking to the rigger if it was the last thing Chelbie did. Mallory knew she might as well come to grips with the idea now.

Maybe it won't sting as much if he shoots me down with Chelbie standing right there.

It would sting regardless, but an embarrassment shared with her best friend was an embarrassment more easily gotten over, she supposed.

* * * *

When Scrye and June took their first break, Kel used that opportunity to swap out camera batteries. He'd stupidly forgotten to recharge them the night before. That was one reason he always carried plenty of extras. Some of the attendees crowded around Scrye and June, asking questions about the ties he'd used, putting Kel's friend firmly in his element as the center of attention and praise.

Kel was focused on one of his cameras when he heard a woman clear her throat behind him. He turned to see the young woman with the red pixie cut. Just behind her, her friend, the gorgeous woman who'd captured his attention earlier.

He straightened and smiled. "Hi."

Pixie Cut grinned. "Hiya. I'm Chelbie." She hooked a thumb over her shoulder at her friend. "This is my bestie, Mallory. I'm that annoying kind of friend who will force you to get over whatever you're embarrassed about. She would really like to experience rope, but she's been too chickenshit to approach any of the riggers about it."

He glanced over her shoulder to see Mallory's face now practically glowing red. In fact, it looked like she was about to turn and run, but Chelbie's right hand shot out behind her and unerringly captured her friend's left wrist, preventing her escape.

He offered up a smile. "You've never been tied before?"

Mallory's gaze dropped to the floor. He took the barely perceptible movement of her head as a negatory.

Okay, so my way to her is through the friend.

He wasn't an idiot.

"Are you two coming back here tonight for the play session?" he asked.

Chelbie's grin broadened. "Oh, absolutely. Can't wait."

"Good. Why don't you two come to dinner with us, and while we're eating, we can talk about it and decide what you'd like to try?"

Mallory looked up at him, her eyes as wide as dessert plates before her gaze dropped to the floor again.

Chelbie yanked Mallory forward so she stood next to her. "Thank you! We'd *love* to."

"It's at Sigalo's. My treat," he added before Mallory could object. "And it won't be just the three of us. There will probably be about ten of us or so. If that's all right?"

"That sounds mahhhvelous," Chelbie said, pumping Mallory's arm as if trying to work a recalcitrant ventriloquist dummy. "And I know where that is, too. What time?"

"Seven."

"Egggcellent," Chelbie said. He couldn't decide if she was normally that upbeat and gregarious, or putting on a show to try to get her obviously mortified friend to smile.

He extended his hand to Mallory, his gaze focused solely on her, mentally willing her to look up at him again. "I'd be honored to pop your rope cherry," he joked, hoping she took it in the playful way he'd meant it.

"Mal," Chelbie said. "This is where you take his hand and shake with him, babe."

Mallory slowly raised her head just enough that she could cover the rest of the distance by glancing up at him with those gorgeous blue eyes of hers. Her grip felt cool and the slightest bit trembly in his.

"Thank you," she quietly said.

* * * *

Mallory hoped she didn't puke all over the guy's sneakers.
I. Am. Going. To. Fucking. Kill. Her.
She knew it. She just *knew* Chelbie wouldn't leave it alone.

Kel didn't release her hand, apparently waiting for something. When she forced herself to look up at him again, he said, "I mean it. If I'd known you were interested in being tied, I would have approached you a long time ago."

She didn't know if he was humoring her or not, then decided she didn't want to know. At least for tonight, it would seem, she might get to have one damn good thing happen.

"I know I'm not exactly your type," she said before thinking about it.

Chelbie's fingers painfully dug into her left wrist, but Kel still didn't let go of her right hand.

"What do you think my 'type' is?" he asked, no trace of sarcasm in his tone.

She took a deep breath and, low enough others around them couldn't hear, she said, "I know you usually tie skinny girls."

Now his grip grew a little firmer. "My type," he said, "is anyone willing to be tied, whom I can do so safely. Do you have any issues, like a back injury, that would prevent me from tying you in any particular way?"

She shook her head. "I'm just, you know, fat."

She'd glanced away but he still didn't release her hand. He seemed to be waiting for her to look up at him again.

She finally did. Something about the intensity of his brown gaze pierced right through her. "I see you as a beautiful, blank canvas that I can't wait to take control of."

Her mouth went dry. Chelbie leaned in and *sotto voce* said, "If you don't let him tie you tonight, I will beat you myself in the bad way for committing acts of terminal stupidity."

Kel smiled, brought her hand to his lips, and kissed it. A torrent of emotions rushed through her. "We'll talk in detail over dinner," he said, "so that when we return tonight, we won't have to waste our time with that. We can get right to the fun part." One eyebrow deliciously arched at her.

Her clit throbbed in response, shocking her. She knew he was just being nice, trying to make her feel better, but her body didn't care about that.

Her body only cared about how sexy he'd just become to her.

Come on, brain. Take control of this. Last thing I need is unrequited love to fuck up what little normalcy I already have.

"Okay," she said, wanting Chelbie to loosen her death grip on her left hand so the blood flow would return to her fingers. "I'd like that."

Only then did he release her right hand after one final, gentle squeeze. "Good. Because I know I'm looking forward to it. And, for future reference, any time you want to be tied, I hope you'll ask me first. Because I'll never say no to you."

Chelbie leaned in again and whispered in her ear. "*Hah. So there.*"

Chapter Seven

"Explain to me why I shouldn't kill you," Mallory grumbled when they were in the car and on their way to Chelbie's house.

Her friend settled back in the seat, wearing a grin that would put the Cheshire Cat to shame. "Because you looove me. And I just got you a confirmed rigging session with a *really* hot guy. Oh, and farking dinner, thank you very much. You're welcome."

"Thank you," she mumbled.

Impossibly, Chelbie's grin widened. "Anytime. What's a bestie for if not to shove you off the high dive?"

Back at Chelbie's, they both grabbed showers and started getting ready. As it grew closer to time for them to leave, Mallory tried to rein in the frustration and excitement that warred within her. In her hurry to find her makeup, she dumped her purse out on Chelbie's bed.

Her friend reached out and plucked the warning citation, the car registration, insurance card, and Mallory's license from the pile. "What's this?"

"Oh, that's from the cop pulling me over. I meant to put the registration and insurance card back in the glove box. Don't let me forget to do that, please."

Chelbie frowned as she studied the items. "It says the owner of your car is the Mallory Ann Weaver Trust." Chelbie looked up at her. "What the hell does *that* mean?"

Mallory shrugged. "I don't know." She retrieved her license from Chelbie and tucked it back into her wallet. "When he bought me the car, that's what he had it put under. I figured it probably had something to do with my trust." The Honda Civic had been four years old when he'd bought it for her when she turned seventeen, but it had low miles and was in excellent condition.

One of the few times she could count that he'd taken the initiative and purchased something for her without her having to ask for it.

"Did you ever find out how much is left in the trust account?"

"No. He won't discuss it with me."

Chelbie cocked her head, looking a little like a puzzled terrier. "Don't you think that's just a little bit strange? Why the hell won't you let me talk to my parents about getting you an attorney? I'm sure there's something *really* wrong going on here."

"It's supposed to be some standard thing people do all the time. Reduces liability. Especially for cars. I just haven't been in the mood to fight him on it lately. We fight enough as it is."

"Well, does your uncle have his own trust?"

"I—" She snapped her mouth shut on that answer. "I don't know. I figured he probably does."

"Didn't you mention something happened a few years ago when your grandfather died?"

Her uncle hadn't been close to his father at all, meaning she'd had very little chance to get to know him. Her uncle had flown up to New Jersey for the funeral, leaving her with Chelbie's parents for the week while he handled whatever he had to do up there as the sole remaining heir. Her father had been the youngest, her uncle the oldest. There'd been a sister who'd died before Mallory's birth, from an asthma attack when she'd been a teenager.

At the time of her grandfather's death, Mallory had been a junior in high school, and it was mid-term exam time. She'd wanted to go with him, if nothing else to meet other people in their extended family, but he'd insisted she stay home and take her exams.

A week later, a FedEx box had arrived from a law firm in New Jersey. Her uncle had her sign a couple of forms she didn't understand.

But at the time she'd been too busy trying to avoid him, or the inevitable fights with him, or was involved with her studies, to dig any deeper.

"I don't know," Mallory admitted. "Maybe. I never really looked into it."

Chelbie's head cocked to the other side. "I think it's time you quit avoiding the inevitable. Don't you? What about the bank accounts? You have a right to see what's in them."

"He transfers my expense allowance every week into my personal account. Or if I need something for school, or car repairs, or whatever."

Even as she said it, she felt stupid.

Chelbie returned the paperwork to her. "Next week we'll deal with that. Tonight is about having fun. We're going to go out to dinner with everyone, go to the club, and you're going to spend the night here with me. My parents are out of town for the weekend, so you have no excuses about how late we stay out. Not that they care anyway, as long as I give them a heads-up so they don't worry."

Mallory drew in a deep breath and held it before letting it out again. "Did I ever tell you how much I envy you?"

Chelbie threw her arms around her. "You're like the sister I never had. And my 'rents love you. Please, say the word, and you have a home here."

"You've already talked with them about me moving in, haven't you?"

Chelbie laughed as she sat back. "Guilty. Duh." She rested her hands on Mallory's shoulders. "Look, I'm done being the supportive friend. I'm ready to assume the role of ass-riding friend to get you to deal with this stuff. As you witnessed earlier today."

"Why haven't I sicced you on my uncle before now?"

"I don't know. I keep asking you that, and you always have a dumbass excuse. Blah, blah, don't rock the boat. Blah, blah, you don't want to be a bother. Blah, blah, killing him and dumping his body in the Gulf is illegal. Sheesh." Chelbie pulled her in for another hug. "Tonight, we feast, we fun, we frolic. Tomorrow, we fight that fucker."

"Glad you're on my side."

"Babe, I'm *always* on your side."

* * * *

Excitement hummed through Kel in a way he rarely felt anymore as he schlepped his equipment back to his apartment.

Dinner with the two women would be wonderful.

Especially with Mallory.

It wasn't the first time he'd seen a woman emotionally crippled by a poor body image when it came to participating in lifestyle activities.

But he'd also personally witnessed many of those same women come to flourish, grow confident, feel sexy, transform their outlook, and start to see themselves as the beautiful women others already saw.

A point in Mallory's favor, he'd never heard of her being involved in any drama around the club. As far as he knew, she wasn't in a relationship. If she was, they never came to the club with her.

Someone new to rope, who'd never been tied before, who might be drama-free and single?

Yes, please.

That he found himself attracted to her and barely knew her was a plus. He hoped as he grew to know her better that his first impression of her wouldn't be blown out of the water by a cold torpedo of reality.

That would suck.

By the time he arrived fifteen minutes early at the restaurant, he'd showered, shaved, and changed into the jeans and black, button-up shirt he planned on wearing to the club. His rope and rigging bags were in the truck, so he didn't have to go back to his place to get them.

He wanted to try to time their arrival at the club to be there as soon as they opened, when they were still fairly slow, and get Mallory as comfortable as possible before tying her. He just hoped he could convince her to play with him for a goodly chunk of the evening, not simply a one-and-done tie before she headed off to play with another Top.

Hell, he hoped Mallory's friend wouldn't let her back out of their dinner commitment. He hadn't exchanged phone numbers with them while at the demo, and they'd left before he'd had a chance to say good-bye.

He suspected Mallory had bodily dragged Chelbie out of there and probably chewed her out all the way home.

He smiled. He had lots of friends, good friends, but it seemed Chelbie crossed the line into soul sister with Mallory, from what he'd witnessed in the short amount of time he'd talked with them. Thinking back on other times he'd seen them at the club, it seemed like he remembered Chelbie keeping a close eye on Mallory while her friend scened with Tops. In fact, he couldn't remember seeing Mallory at the club that Chelbie wasn't by her side.

The women arrived right on time, about the same time Tony and Shayla pulled into the parking lot. He'd already given his friends the heads-up that they'd have two newbies joining their group for dinner.

As they all gathered and were shown to their reserved table, Kel didn't miss that Chelbie made sure Mallory was seated between himself and her.

* * * *

Mallory wasn't sure if she wanted to kiss or kill Chelbie, but here they were at dinner, regardless. If it'd been up to Mallory, she would have blown it off, as well as going back to the club that night.

No, she didn't get the feeling Kel was going to be mean or embarrass her, but the more she thought about being the focus of attention, the less she wanted to do it. Anytime he started rigging, a large group gathered around to watch.

That was something she didn't know if she could handle.

Once their orders were in, Kel focused on her again. "Did you grow up in Sarasota?"

"Sort of. Mostly. I was born in Rapid City, but I've been here since I was ten."

"Ah. Your parents moved here?"

"They died," she said. It didn't sting as much to say it like it had in the early days. "My uncle and aunt lived here and they took me in."

"Oh. I'm sorry."

"It's okay." She took a sip of her water. "Damn drunk driver. They had gone to a friend's birthday party at a restaurant, and were on their way home when it happened. My neighbor was babysitting when the cops showed up at the house."

"My dad was killed by a drunk, too," he said.

She stared at him. "Really?"

He nodded. "He was a truck driver. Asshole going the wrong way on I-275 up in Tampa one night. He flipped the rig trying to avoid them. Got trapped in the cab and burned."

"That's horrible. How old were you?"

"Seventeen. Fifteen years later, and my mom still can't get past it in some ways. I've tried to talk her into getting out and meeting people, but she can't make herself do it yet."

"I'm sorry. Horrible club to be a member of, huh?"

"Yeah. Needless to say, I'm not a drinker."

She smiled. "Neither am I."

"See? Something else we have in common." He held his glass of iced tea up and she gently clinked her water glass against it. "To teetotalers," he said.

* * * *

Kel desperately wanted to get off the topic of their common tragedy. Dwelling on it wouldn't exactly foster a mindset that would promote a good, sexy scene later. "So are you still in college?" he asked.

"Yes. Two more semesters at Ringling. Graphic design."

Yay! Another common topic that wasn't macabre. "Really? Tell me more." As she talked, he saw signs of her loosening up, relaxing around him.

He also noted how her friend noticeably backed off, too, chatting with others around the table even as she seemed to keep an ear on their conversation.

"I'd love to see your portfolio," he said, genuinely interested in her work.

Without a word, Chelbie reached back and fumbled around in Mallory's purse, found her friend's phone, and quickly swiped through it before handing it over to him. "She's too modest," Chelbie said before returning to her conversation with Tilly about some book series.

Mallory's cheeks pinkened up a little, but she didn't retreat. "Did I mention my best friend's crazy?" she muttered, smiling.

He grinned, leaning in so Mallory could actually see the phone and direct the discussion, tell him about her different art pieces as he looked at the pictures. By the time their food arrived, Kel found himself not only impressed by the quality of Mallory's work, but entranced by her as a person. She was just about to put her phone up when it chimed in her hand.

She quickly silenced the text message alert, frowning as she started to shove the phone back into her purse.

Lightning-fast Chelbie once again interceded. "Uh, no he *didn't*," she said, snatching the phone from her friend as she read the text message.

Kel tried not to let his hopes sink a little. "Is everything okay?"

"Her stupid uncle," Chelbie said as she swiped the text message clear and returned the phone to her friend's purse. "He's an asshat." She proceeded to give an abbreviated and extremely one-sided version of events as only a dedicated friend could.

As Kel listened, he hoped he didn't have to revise his opinion of Mallory's drama-free status. She was single, a point in her favor.

"Hold on," Seth said from across the table. He'd apparently caught part of the conversation. "Sorry to eavesdrop, but did you say her uncle won't go through the trust paperwork with her?"

"Exactly!" Chelbie said, and then she was off to the races again, launching into a more detailed diatribe as Mallory sat there growing progressively more red in the face.

Kel couldn't help it. He reached over, found her hand under the table, and gently squeezed. She threw him a grateful glance that made him want to take up the banner of whatever problem this was on her behalf.

When Chelbie finished the detailed version of events, Seth's wife, Leah, looked at him. "We could call Ed for her. See if he'll look into it."

"I can't afford an attorney," Mallory said.

"I'm sure he'd give you a free consultation," Seth said.

"Not knowing all the details," Tony added, "I'd have to agree with your friend here. It sounds to me like something isn't right. Or at the very least, your uncle is hiding something from you."

"A trust like that," Ross chimed in, "would likely go to you at age eighteen or twenty-one. Those are two pretty standard benchmarks."

Mallory seemed to grow increasingly uncomfortable with all their attention, good intentions or not, focused on her. "I know. I just haven't had the time or energy to fight him on it yet," she said. "I didn't mean to derail the conversation. Sorry."

"I think *I* derailed the conversation," Chelbie said. "At least now you know it's not just me thinking something stinks."

Mallory's discomfort washed off her in waves. Kel squeezed her hand one final time before releasing it. "Sorry. Didn't mean to put you in the spotlight," he said. "Let's get back to talking about rope."

She gratefully nodded and picked up her fork. She'd only ordered a salad for her entrée despite him encouraging her to order whatever she wanted.

At one point, she excused herself to the bathroom. Kel thought Chelbie would get up and go with her, but she remained in her seat, watching until her friend was out of sight.

Then she leaned in toward Kel. "You know what that fucker texted her?" she whispered.

"Who?"

"Her damn uncle."

"What?"

"He demanded to know where she was, and that she come home immediately to talk about her grad school application. I'm telling you, the guy is whacked. Thank you for helping me pummel that through her brain. I don't think she wants to make waves, but I'm about ready to move her out of there my damn self if I have to." She reached for her own phone and started texting. "And I'm going to tell him off."

He reached out and touched her hand. "You sure that's wise?"

"I know that whatever's going on, it started when Mallory hit eighteen. I'm not talking parental concern. I'm talking obsessive movie-of-the-week creepy." Her fingers flew over her screen. "There." She hit send.

"What'd you text him?"

"I told him that Mal was with me, and she would be spending the night with me, and that we are out with friends." She grinned as she slipped the phone back into her purse. "And that he could kiss my lily white ass if he doesn't like it."

She fished Mallory's phone out of her purse and waited, then grinned as she intercepted a call and sent it straight to voice mail. She glanced up, watching for Mallory. A voice message must have appeared, because Chelbie thumbed that, then deleted it.

Then she turned off the ringer and tucked Mallory's phone into her own purse. "I'm sure he'll be plenty pissed off by tomorrow night. Maybe enough to bring things to a head."

"I don't ever want you mad at me."

She grinned. "You're right. You don't."

Chapter Eight

Mallory realized as they were leaving the restaurant that her phone wasn't in her purse. When she stopped in the foyer and shot Chelbie a warning look, Chelbie shot one back that cowed her.

"You don't get your phone back tonight, girlie," she said. "I shall take charge of it for you. No Uncle Buzzkill to upset you tonight."

"Why? Did he say something else besides that text?"

"Does it matter if he did or didn't?" She hooked her arm through Mallory's and started leading her out to the car. "All I know is I'm happy with what you and Kel talked about. If I didn't know firsthand that the guy knows his rope, I would still be happy with you playing with him tonight. You're going to relax and have fun and feel safe and know that I've got your back."

Kel had hung back, talking with Seth and a couple of others. Now he caught up with them, giving Mallory a playful smile that threatened to melt her panties.

"Okay, so on to the club," he said, pointing at her. "You are the only person on my dance card tonight, as far as I'm concerned. As long as you want to play, we'll play. Deal?"

She nodded, not even needing Chelbie's friendly poke in the side. "Deal."

"Good. Thank you for trusting me," he said. "I'll do my best not to let you down."

"Thank you."

Chelbie had driven them to the restaurant in her car, a yellow VW Bug Mallory adored even though it felt tiny and cramped compared to her four-door Honda Civic. "Do I need to give you an additional pep talk before we get there," Chelbie asked, "or are you good to go?"

"I'm good to go. I think. I hope."

"Stop it. If I didn't think he was being sincere, do you think I'd let you play with him?"

"You are going to make someone a wonderful drill sergeant when you get married, you know that?"

She grinned. "I think the words you're looking for are *overprotective* and *snarky*."

"Those will work," Mallory agreed.

Mallory had opted to wear a black maxi skirt and a colorful blouse that didn't make her stand out too much. She only owned one corset, a black one, that while she liked it, it was uncomfortable as hell to wear for too long.

Kel pulled into the club's parking lot right behind them, leaving Mallory no chance to talk Chelbie into letting her flee.

Then again, when she got another look at the man, did she *really* want to run? She'd never seen him pull any pranks or act mean to anyone at the club. Had never heard anything bad about him. From their talk at dinner, he genuinely seemed to want to play with her.

Why, she had no clue.

What do you call a pity fuck that doesn't actually involve fucking?

They checked in with the staffer manning the front desk, paid their entry fee, and followed Kel into the playspace. Tonight it looked different, the overhead lights turned off, and in their place various colored lights and soft spots illuminating the playspace and straddling the fine line between safely lit and mood lighting. There were already a few people there, some she recognized, some she didn't.

Chelbie took her hand and squeezed it. "Relax," her friend said. "Tonight is about fun. Fun, fun, fun."

"That's what you keep saying."

"And I'll keep saying it until you're having it."

The large suspension frame Scrye had used earlier lay vacant. Kel carried his bags over there, and Mallory, led by Chelbie, followed.

He turned to her and offered her a kind smile. "Okay, for starters, do you have any objections to me touching you?"

Chelbie took Mallory's purse off her arm and backed away, sitting by one of the frame's uprights to watch.

Mallory shook her head. "No. I mean, for tying. I don't play…sexually," she finally forced out of her mouth.

He smiled. "Gotcha. Incidental contact is okay, outright groping isn't."

* * * *

Kel struggled to keep his cock under control. As Mal nodded, her face filled with that gorgeous pink flush again. He had her hold out her arms so he could assess her upper body strength and then palpate her shoulders, hips, and ribcage through her clothes.

"Is that an underwire bra?"

"Yes?"

"Do you have something else you can change into? Or would you be okay with me tying you topless? I'm afraid that will cut into you in a bad way if I tie over the top of it."

She looked like she was going to burst into tears. "You know, it's okay. I didn't think about that, I usually only play with—"

"How about I give her my shirt?" Chelbie called out. She wore a black tank top over her bra. "I don't mind walking around with the girls out."

While Kel would have paid money to see the fabric of Chelbie's shirt tightly stretched across Mallory's breasts, he could tell from Mallory's reaction that it wouldn't be an option, either.

Inspiration struck. "Ha. Hold on." He unbuttoned his shirt, stripped off his undershirt, and handed it to her. "There. Problem solved."

The added personal satisfaction of her wearing his T-shirt only added to his fun.

She held on to it for a second, as if trying to decide how to say no before she finally nodded. "Okay. Let me go put it on." She dashed off before he could say anything else.

Chelbie giggled from her spot by the upright as Kel pulled his shirt back on and buttoned it. "Oh, my gawd, chief. Step up your game a little. That was a good move, but she's like a scared rabbit."

He walked over to Chelbie and looked down at her. She didn't flinch, didn't seem the slightest bit fazed. "I'm not trying to play her," he insisted.

"I know, and *that's* the problem." She pointed at his jeans. "Dude, that's either a hard cock, or you're the butchest damn lesbian I've ever seen and packing a massive plastic dong in there. I could feel the electricity between the two of you at dinner. I watched you watching her this afternoon. Sneaking little glances at her when you were supposed to be taking pictures. Buck up, buttercup. I'm cheering for whichever team will bat a home run to get her to feel good about herself. You want into the lineup, all you have to do is step up to the plate."

He had no idea how to respond to any of that. Being at a loss for words wasn't something he was used to, either.

The red-haired pixie grinned up at him. "Some people have a hard time getting used to my forthright style of communication."

"No shit."

"Well, I've seen where playing coy and passive-aggressive gets some women. I'd rather go straight for aggressive-aggressive and ditch the passive part."

When Mal returned a moment later wearing his T-shirt, the sight of her took his breath away and kicked all thoughts of his odd conversation with Chelbie out of his head.

She still wore her skirt, but when she returned to the A-frame, she kicked off her sandals, pulled down her skirt, and neatly folded it, laying her blouse and bra on top of the pile by Chelbie.

When she turned back to him, his T-shirt pulled snug across her breasts and the hem hanging down just to her ass, he knew he'd have a hard time focusing on this particular tie. Normally, he could compartmentalize when doing a scene. Unless he was sexually involved with someone, it was stupidly easy for him to focus only on the mechanics of what he was doing and not get hot and bothered.

Mal had him hot and bothered.

Borderline flustered.

Again, not something he was used to feeling.

Finding his calm, peaceful center would prove difficult tonight if he couldn't stop thinking about how gorgeous she looked wearing his T-shirt.

He opened his rope bags and emptied them, quickly organizing the rope by color and length. He knew from the size of the rope braids which coils were of which length. He had a lot more rope back at his apartment, different colors, weights, materials, most of which he reserved for his own photo shoots. Hemp was one of his favorites, but some models didn't like working with it.

Even fewer liked working with the coconut fiber rope that was even coarser than hemp.

For rigging at the club, he used mostly black and red rope, in both quarter-inch and five-sixteenths widths, a multifilament poly that was solid, smooth, didn't stretch too much, and had never let him down. The specialty MFP wasn't like the stiff, plastic rope that could be found in most hardware stores. He ordered it in bulk from an online rope supplier who dealt with the kinky population. He liked the rope especially because he could wash it periodically without ruining it.

He pulled out his rigging ring and hung it from the climbing carabiner already attached to the frame. Then he dragged a chair over and quickly tied a rope anchor around the ring and frame for extra support. Not that he didn't trust the carabiner, which he knew was rated to five hundred pounds, but he believed in a policy of better safe than sorry.

He'd only dropped one person during a suspension, and that had been early on in his training. A carabineer he'd thought had been rated for climbing had failed. Fortunately, she'd landed mostly on him as he'd lunged to catch her. While she'd been uninjured, he'd twisted his back.

Lesson learned.

He knew the carabiner on this frame was rated, because against its black surface he could still see his initials in white paint from when he'd installed it himself a few months back.

Since he frequently used the rig, he made sure to swap the hardware out from time to time.

And still, after pulling the chair away, he reached up, grabbed the ring, and swung from it to ensure it was secure.

That done, he stood before Mal and gently stroked her upper arms. "You all right?"

She nodded.

He smiled. "Nervous?"

She nodded.

"It's okay to be nervous. I just hope *I* don't disappoint *you*."

Apparently that'd been exactly the right thing to say to her, because her eyebrows shot up in surprise. "Disappoint *me*? I think you have that backward."

"You won't disappoint me," he insisted. "I, however, know you watched Scrye the Guy spend a couple of hours tying his wife this afternoon. Those are pretty big shoes to fill. Literally."

She finally smiled. "I've watched you rig before," she softly said. "I think you're better than Scrye."

"Aww, thank you. I appreciate that. Wasn't fishing for a compliment, but I'll take it."

With the ice finally completely broken, he started working on the chest harness first. He wouldn't deny he tied it in such a way as to accentuate and lift her full breasts, her nipples tautly peaked against the fabric of his T-shirt.

That is now my favorite T-shirt.

He took his time, going slower than he normally would both to make sure she was all right and because he selfishly wanted to savor the moment. He wanted this to be special for her, to be fun. To be something she'd enjoy.

Hopefully, something she'd want to repeat with him.

Repeatedly.

Chapter Nine

Despite her initial bout of nerves, Mallory discovered if she focused on the sound of Kel's voice that the noises in the rest of the club seemed to slip away.

"How you doing?" he asked as he tied another rope around her and started forming the hip harness.

She closed her eyes so she couldn't see the people starting to gather a respectful distance around the perimeter of the A-frame. "Green." She snapped her mouth shut on the "Sir" that wanted to follow it right along behind, as if it was the most natural thing in the world to say.

They barely knew each other. She couldn't just start calling him Sir. Hell, she didn't even call most of the Tops she scened with on a regular basis Sir because they weren't her Dominant. She only ever called two of them Sir, men who were much older than her, and only because it felt like they were kinky adopted dads. A sign of respect, not just an honorific or a protocol-driven label.

After what felt like forever, Kel started running ropes through the ring and the rope harnesses tied to her. She wasn't sure exactly what he was doing, because she'd kept her eyes closed for most of it, enjoying the feel of his hands against her, even if it wasn't meant in an intimate way.

I should have told him he could grope me. I'm an idiot.

"Okay," he said, standing in front of her. "I want you to hold on to my shoulders. Keep your feet where they are, and let me guide you. I promise, you won't fall."

She looked into his brown eyes and nodded. In her peripheral vision, she noted that Tony and Seth were now acting as spotters, standing by the frame's uprights, close, but not intrusively so. She wondered if Kel was going to have them help him get her in the air when he slowly started backing away from her. She realized he had a couple of lengths of rope in his hands, and as she started to pitch forward, the harnesses tightened against her as he took the slack out of the suspension ropes.

"You doing okay?"

She nodded. "I'm okay."

"If it hurts, tell me. Don't tough it out just because you think that's what I want to hear. It'll be easy to make an adjustment."

"Okay."

He took another step back. "Pick up one foot."

She did and realized she was now being supported by the ropes.

He took a wrap of rope around his arms and dipped his knees, and she let out a little cry of surprise when she found herself gently swinging back and forth, facedown, completely off the ground.

He took another pull on the ropes and she felt herself rise a few more inches before he secured the ends and double-checked everything.

Then he gently caught her shoulders and knelt in front of her. "You're flying."

She smiled. "I am, aren't I?"

From her spot, Chelbie gave a whoop. "Superman, baby!"

Kel smiled. "You want to?"

She knew what that meant, had seen plenty of other people do it. She nodded, holding her arms out in front of her. He stepped around to her legs, pulled her back, then gave her a hard shove that sent her sailing out into space.

Chelbie cheered. "Whoo! Fly, girlie, fly!"

Kel kept close watch on her to make sure she didn't run the risk of hitting one of the uprights or any of the spectators, but kept pushing her back and forth, spinning her in different directions before sending her out again.

She loved it.

Why did I wait?

This was fan*fucking*tastic. She heard Tony and Seth occasionally reminding people to step back and fending off people who wanted to get close and talk to Kel. Which she thought was odd, because she'd seen him talk to others plenty of times while rigging people, unless it was during a critical point in the tie.

She didn't care.

Whee!

Laughter filled the air and it took her a second to realize it belonged to her.

Best. Night. Ever.

* * * *

Kel surreptitiously checked on Mallory's hands and feet as he spun and pushed her, making sure it didn't feel like her circulation was impeded. After about twenty minutes, he noticed her wiggling a little, as if trying to get comfortable. That's when he stepped in, putting his arms around her, making her hold on to his shoulders again.

"How we doing?"

Her brilliant smile, her sparkling blue eyes, he wanted to let her fly all night but knew her body would begin to protest at some point, if it wasn't already.

"I think I'm ready to get down."

He gave her a smile in return. "Had enough?"

"It's starting to get a little pinchy. And I'm sure others want to play."

"Don't worry about others. My focus is on you."

"Thank you for this."

"Like I told you, I'll never say no to you. This was a privilege." He unfastened the suspension ropes and slowly belayed her down, until she had her feet under her.

"Don't let go of me yet," he said as he worked to untie the suspension ropes from her harness.

"Why not?"

He smiled. "Because I want to make sure you're steady. I would feel horrible if I got you down safely just to have you crash on me because I didn't pay attention."

Chelbie had already fetched a towel and light fleece throw blanket from the supply of them the club provided and swooped in when he motioned to her to drape the blanket around Mallory.

"Take her to one of the couches and make sure there's room for all three of us. I'll be there in a minute."

"What about the harnesses?" Chelbie asked.

"I want to clear the rig." He quickly coiled and gathered his other ropes. He'd leave the ring up, at least for now, and let someone else use it. Some riggers didn't bring their own rings and it always made him nervous watching people rely solely on a carabiner. When others tried to get his attention to talk, likely to ask for a turn with him, he politely held up a hand and pointed to where Chelbie had gotten Mallory settled on one of the aftercare couches.

Others might think his scene was done, but he wasn't.

Not by a long shot. The energy exchange he'd experienced during their tie had felt like nothing he'd experienced in a long, long time. Crisp, fresh, joyful. Beyond the rote mechanics of the tie and the pride in a job well done and another happy customer, so to speak.

He had felt vested, immersed, drawn into it with her, the rest of the club and attendees fading away outside his range of perception until she was the sole focus and content of his universe.

He grabbed his bags and headed over to the couch, even happier when Mallory nestled against his side when he sat next to her and draped his arm around her shoulders.

"So?" he asked.

Eyes closed, she wore a dreamy smile he suspected was one of her subspace tells. She nodded. "Thank you."

"Oh, that's so cute. You think you're done."

Chelbie let out a snort but didn't say anything. It was a common line amongst many of the Tops at their club.

"We're not?" Mallory asked.

"Well, not unless you want to go home wearing a rope harness, no."

Actually the thought of her doing just that, wearing not just his T-shirt home but his ropes, too, threatened to stiffen his cock again.

"Oh." She sounded a little disappointed.

He coaxed her into lying on her back, her head in his lap, her legs draped over Chelbie. Lacing his fingers through hers, he gave her hand a gentle squeeze. "Doesn't mean we can't do other ties tonight. I'll even fly you again, if you want."

* * * *

Mallory opened her eyes to find herself staring into Kel's brown gaze. When had she ended up in his lap? She didn't know and didn't care.

She also didn't want to read more into this. Because she knew damn well he didn't usually do aftercare on his rope bottoms. Many didn't even need it, but the few who did, normally their partners or friends shuttled them off to take care of it.

Yet, here he was.

Holding. My. Hand.

Her thoughts swirled, eddied, flowed, emotions bubbling and bursting and retreating as she struggled to deal with this.

Oooh, yeah. I'm deep.

She'd never recalled hitting subspace this hard before with anyone else. And she didn't even hit subspace on a reliable basis. Sometimes she did, sometimes she didn't.

This was…

Sigh.

She could stay curled up in Kel's lap all night. Would, too, if he let her.

When she started to sit up a few minutes later, painfully aware that she was now hogging his time, he laid his other hand on her shoulder to stay her movements.

"No rush," he said. "Let's just chill out."

Well, I'm dang sure not going to argue.

Chapter Ten

Kel didn't play with anyone else that night but her. Mallory didn't know if he was trying to be nice or genuinely had wanted to play with her.

For the sake of her dignity, she'd take him at his word that he was having as much fun as she was.

After untying the chest and hip harnesses, he'd sat there with her on the couch, showing her other ties, working with her, joking around and keeping her laughing.

It was a night she'd cherish in her memories.

When Mallory and Chelbie finally returned to Chelbie's house a little after 2:00 am, Mallory hunted for her cell phone again just to remember Chelbie had it.

"Dammit, I forgot my charger."

"I'll put it on mine for you," Chelbie told her. "Just go to bed and don't worry about reality."

She leaned against the doorway of Chelbie's room. "Do you think he had fun?"

"Who, Kel?"

"Yeah."

Chelbie arched an eyebrow at her. "I think the man was damn sure enjoying himself. I watched him while he flew you. I think his smile was nearly as big as yours. He was really getting off on how much fun you were having."

"I know I shouldn't read anything into that."

"Then don't. Take it for what it was, a great night." She smiled. "And take the man at his word that he wants to play with you again.

He doesn't strike me as the type to say something like that if he doesn't mean it."

"I'm so tired and brain-fried I'm going to agree with you without argument."

"I think Hell just froze over." But Chelbie grinned. "Now go get some sleep."

Mallory awakened late the next morning in the guest room of Chelbie's house and experienced a moment of disorientation before the events of the previous night came flooding back to her.

Shivering, she rubbed her hands up and down her arms, wishing the textured ligature marks had lasted throughout the night. She held her arms up and stared at them, where the ropes had been, spotting no sign of bruising.

Damn.

She loved having marks. It was always a visual reminder to her of the play, of the feelings she'd experienced, the blissful calm that inhabited her brain during those short mental vacations.

She wished Kel had marked her.

In a way that would have lasted more than an hour or two.

She got up to use the bathroom, meeting up with Chelbie in the hallway.

"How you doing?" Chelbie asked her.

Mallory nodded, smiling before bursting into unexpected tears.

Chelbie shuttled her into her room and down onto the bed. "Hey, what's wrong?"

"I..." She shrugged, then shook her head, and shrugged again.

Chelbie gently laughed as she held her. "It was that good, huh?"

"Yeah."

Her friend slowly rocked her, comforting her. "It's okay. Get it out of your system and don't try to hold it in. We'll get ourselves showered and dressed and go out for a little pancake coma action to combat your subdrop. How's that sound?"

Mallory nodded.

"Good. I'll—"

They both looked up at the sound of Mallory's phone ringing from on top of the dresser, where Chelbie had plugged it into her charger when they returned home. Before Mallory could react, Chelbie had reached for it, frowning, then grinning when she looked at the screen and answered.

"Hi, Kel." Chelbie backed away as Mallory lunged, trying to wrest the phone from her. "How are you this morning?" Chelbie held an arm out, leaning back just out of Mallory's reach. "We just got up and were discussing going out for brunch. I think she's a little subdroppy. Would you like to join us?"

Mallory flopped onto the bed, mortified.

"That would be fan*tas*tic," Chelbie said. She gave him her address. "We'll be ready when you get here. See you then." She ended the call and dropped the phone onto the mattress beside her friend. "You're welcome. Get up and get moving. He'll be here in thirty minutes."

"I am going to kill you," Mallory mumbled into the mattress.

Chelbie leaned in and kissed her cheek. "No you won't. You *looove* me. Just promise me if I meet a guy and have trouble saying hi to him that you'll kick me in the ass and make it happen."

Mallory sat up. "Why did you tell him I'm dropping?"

Chelbie sank down onto the bed next to her. Her tone gentled. "Because you are," she said. "I've seen you get a little droppy before, but not this bad. I can see it in your face, in your body language. And the crying, duh. As your bestie, trust me when I say we need to nip this in the bud before you get too deep. Hey, he sounded very concerned when he asked how you were, even before I told him. Humor me." She stood and started gathering stuff for her shower. "I'll shower in my 'rents' bathroom. You take mine. Chop-chop, girlie. Time's ticking."

There wasn't anything to do but let Chelbie have her way.

Denying she wanted to see Kel would have been a damned lie, anyway.

They were ready to go when he arrived. Chelbie settled the matter of what vehicle they'd take by declaring Mallory had shotgun in Kel's truck and making a beeline for the backseat of the extended cab.

Mallory's face flushed as Kel took her hands. "You all right?" he asked.

"I'm…yeah. I'll be okay."

"Ignore her," Chelbie called from the backseat. "She doesn't want to admit she's dropping."

Mallory risked a glance up into his face and spotted a warm, kind smile.

He squeezed her hands, holding them against his chest. "If you two aren't busy this afternoon, I'd really like to go back to the club and work with you some more."

"But they're closed today."

"Well, since I happen to be the landlord, and I happen to have a key to the place, *and* I happen to be best friends with the owner and have his permission to use it anytime I need it, I'd say it'll be all right. What do *you* say? Please? Sometimes a little hair of the dog helps derail subdrop."

"She says yes," Chelbie called out. "Let's go eat. Pancakes are calling my name in a loud and lonely way."

Mallory nodded. "Okay. Thank you." It would be a great excuse to not think about whatever shitstorm awaited her when she finally forced herself to return home.

He pulled her in for a hug and it took every ounce of her will not to melt against his body and start crying right there. Usually she only got this emotional after fighting with her uncle. The rest of her life, normally, she could deal with anything else in a fairly straightforward way.

"I don't want you to think I'm creeping on you," he said, low enough Chelbie couldn't overhear. "I mean it. But I'd like to get to know you better and spend more time with you. I had fun last night, and I really enjoyed scening with you."

He sounded sincere. "Thank you. I did, too."

"Good." He finally released her. "Let's go grab a bite to eat and then we can go have a relaxing afternoon." They got into his truck.

"Oh, thank gaaawwd," Chelbie said. "I thought she'd never chill out and get past her fear with you." She leaned forward over the seat back. "I know your rep, dude," she said. "You're a good guy. That's why I trust you with her. You hurt her in the bad way? They'll never find your body."

Mallory groaned as she fastened her seat belt. "Did I warn you my best friend is an overprotective whacko?"

He smiled. "The best friends usually are," he said.

Chelbie grinned. "*Hah*," she said to Mallory before she sat back and fastened her seat belt.

* * * *

Kel had spent a restless night trying to sleep, unsuccessful at getting thoughts of Mal out of his mind.

Even when he did fall asleep, he dreamed about her, of having her naked, his ropes on her, and…more.

Marking her.

Owning her.

Taking her sweet, creamy flesh and turning her into his canvas.

Even rubbing one out in the shower when he got up hadn't helped take his mind off her. He didn't want to call her too early to check up on her, wake her up, but finally, around eleven, he couldn't make himself wait any longer. He'd have to risk pissing her off by waking her up.

He'd been a little surprised when Chelbie had answered, then delighted to be invited to brunch with them.

And protectively concerned when Chelbie told him Mal was going through subdrop. He'd worried she might from how deep she'd gone into subspace the night before and how long she'd stayed there.

What he wanted to do was curl up in a bed with her and hold her, soothe her, comfort her.

I really *have got to get a handle on this.*

He barely knew her. She barely knew him. Considering what he'd gone through with Krystal, jumping into a relationship with someone he just met was out of the question. And he wasn't a casual sex kind of guy, either. If he couldn't have a relationship with someone, he wasn't interested in just a one-night stand with them.

Mallory was someone he suspected he could have a relationship with.

Anything worth having is worth waiting for.

Breakfast was wonderful. When they returned to the club, Mallory pulled his T-shirt out of her bag. "I'm sorry I forgot to give this back to you last night."

He smiled. "You can wear it again today, if you'd like."

The smile she gave him in return lit his soul.

While she changed, he went into the office and pulled up his personal playlist on the club's computer and turned on the sound system. Steely Dan softly filled the air. Today would be about getting to know Mallory better. Letting her get to know him.

And, hopefully, cementing the start of what might turn into a relationship.

Chelbie sat across the space, on one of the couches, working on her laptop and not really paying attention to what the two of them were doing. Fine by him, because he wanted Mal's entire focus on him.

He started with them both sitting, playing with some more artistic ties he usually didn't use in the normal course of rigging at the club. They took longer to tie, and while functional, he usually had too many people waiting for a turn to spend the extra time being fancy.

"It's nice not to have to rush," he said.

She looked up into his face. "I hope I'm not keeping you from work or anything," she softly said.

"Not at all. If it hadn't been for this, I'd just be sitting around and watching TV or reading today. I try to take at least one day off a week to recharge. Being self-employed, sometimes it feels like I work harder, and more hours, than I ever did working for someone else."

"I hope I can get to the point someday that I can be self-employed."

"You've got the talent. Your work is amazing. Sometimes I get requests from customers to do things I can't and have to farm out." He made a point of meeting her gaze, unblinking. "Now I know who to call to bring in to do that for me."

"Who?"

He reached out and gently touched the tip of her nose. "Silly."

She lit up, gorgeous. "Thank you."

He suspected from her tone of voice that she still surfed the edge of subspace a little. That she felt that depth of rapport with him didn't help him hold his lizard brain in check.

From across the room, Mal's phone rang in her purse. Chelbie dove for it before Mal could even react.

"Oh, no you don't," Chelbie called out, holding it up after she'd silenced it. "You keep your tushy right there with Kel. Real world isn't allowed in here today."

When Mal pulled her focus back to him, a dark cloud of worry seemed to have settled over her that hadn't been there moments before. "Are you all right?" he asked.

She shrugged. "It was probably my uncle, wanting to know where I am."

"Worried about you?"

"Hah. Not likely. More worried about my nonexistent grad school application. I told him yesterday that I wouldn't be home until late today." Her gaze dropped to her hands, which lay clasped in her lap.

"I really need to nut up and move out. I keep making excuses to myself. But I know everyone's right. I need to figure out how to hire an attorney and find out what's left in the trust, if anything, and move out so I can be done with him."

Kel went out on a limb. "Would you and Chelbie like to have dinner with me tonight? Next door at my place. I'll cook."

Her gaze rose to meet his again. "You live next door?"

"I thought everyone knew that." He pointed a finger at the club's back wall. "On the other side. I have an upstairs apartment."

He didn't know where her hesitation sprang from. He finally added, "I meant what I said. I'd like to spend time getting to know you."

"Say yes," Chelbie called out from the other side of the room. He hadn't realized she'd been able to hear them, much less had been listening to them.

Mal smiled. "Yes."

"Atta girl," Chelbie said.

Chapter Eleven

They spent several hours at the club. The more time Mallory spent talking with Kel, just being around him, the more his calm energy settled and relaxed her.

She was even able to not think about going home later that night.

Add in the fact that Mallory couldn't have loved Chelbie any more for the way she mostly stayed quiet and out of the way, yet providing that extra layer of emotional security, and it was a perfect afternoon.

When Kel finally called it a day with the ropes, they helped him pack them up, learning how he made the rope braids that kept them from getting tangled. She wasn't sure what to expect when they climbed into his truck for the short drive around to his apartment. When he unlocked the door and they walked in, the office looked neat and tidy, not homey, but almost as if a staged scene out of an IKEA brochure or something. Two desks formed an L in one corner, with three large monitors, a desktop, and a laptop residing there. A three-drawer file cabinet held a regular printer, while a table on the other side of the desks held what looked like a large, professional-grade photo printer.

Framed pictures hung on the walls, everything from gorgeous nature shots to tasteful bondage scenes.

"Wow." She walked over to one. It was a close-up of what looked like a woman's lower arm, coils of blue rope still wrapped around her, but fresh ligature marks left behind just above them. "This is beautiful."

"Thank you. Some of my favorites. I love playing with textures and patterns in my photography."

He led them upstairs. The apartment was as neat and tidy as the office. He waved them toward the sofa in front of the TV. "Feel free to put the TV on any channel you like. I'm going to change. I'll be right back."

When they heard the door shut down the hall, Chelbie leaned in. "Okay, I'm going to say this right now. If you don't chase his ass, I'm going to."

"Shh!" Horrified, Mallory glanced over her shoulder to make sure they were still alone.

"I mean it," she said. "He's giving you all the signs. Kudos to him for wanting to take it slow. Let. It. Happen." She frowned. "Unless you aren't attracted to him."

Heat filled Mallory's face. "I am," she whispered, "but do we have to talk about this tonight? Or here?"

Chelbie grinned. "Nope. Just wanted to make sure I was reading the signs right."

* * * *

Kel threw on a pair of shorts and a T-shirt. Before he left his bedroom, he grabbed the T-shirt Mal had worn, which she'd returned to him a few minutes earlier, and inhaled. It still felt a little warm from her body.

And now it smelled like her, sweet and delicious.

Dammit.

He knew he had it bad.

Slow down. Take your time. No rush.

He'd always silently scoffed at people in the lifestyle who jumped head over teacup into a new relationship within days—or sooner—of meeting someone. They almost always flamed out in a spectacular way, like a dragster exploding as it sped toward the finish line.

Usually maiming hearts in the process, and sometimes taking friendships with it as people took sides.

Yes, he'd felt passing attraction to women before. This was more. This felt deeper. This was beyond anything he could remember experiencing, a visceral level sparkle that left him wanting to keep Mallory around as long as possible, reluctant to let her go.

It was also something he'd never felt for Krystal, his ex.

He cooked them an easy meal of spaghetti and homemade meatballs. They ate at his small, four-person dinette, and he tried to drag the evening out as long as he could. They helped him clean up. Then they sat on the couch and talked while the TV played on, ignored.

Finally, Mal let out a yawn around nine o'clock. "Sorry," she said.

"It's all right. I hope you're feeling better, though."

"I am. Thank you."

He took her hand in his, holding it against his chest, not wanting to give her up. "Next Saturday, would you like to get together? Dinner and then the club?"

Her smile lit his soul. "I'd love that. Thank you."

Chelbie grinned. "Why don't you pick her up for dinner? I'll meet you at the restaurant."

Mal looked at her friend. "What? Meet us there? Why not come with us?"

"Oh, come on. Seriously? You don't need a chaperone every time you two get together. If he was a serial killer, he would have offed us by now. Either of us disappear, our DNA is all over the dang place." She smiled at him. "No offense. Not saying I think you're a killer, mind you."

He laughed. "No offense taken." He admired Chelbie, could see why Mal loved her. She was a fiercely protective and loving friend who was probably one of the few tethers to normalcy in Mal's life. Based on what he'd learned about Mal's uncle, Chelbie was probably the closest thing to real family Mal had, too, in terms of emotional and loving support.

"You didn't confirm it for him, girlie," Chelbie chided. "When I said he could pick you up."

"Yes," Mal said. "I'd love that."

He kissed her hand. "I'd love that, too."

He drove them back to Chelbie's house and walked them to the front door. There was another car in the driveway that hadn't been there earlier when he'd picked them up.

"The 'rents have safely returned," Chelbie said. She stuck out her hand to Kel. "Thank you, dude. This was a great day. I'll leave you two alone to say good night."

After Chelbie slipped inside and shut the door, Mal turned to him. "I really did have fun. Thank you."

He wanted to lean in, grab her, and kiss her, hard and deep.

Taking a deep breath, he reined in that urge and leaned in to place a sweet, tender kiss on her forehead. "I loved it, too. I want you to text me this week. Or call me if you need to talk. Promise?"

"I don't want to bother you."

"Stop that. It's not a bother. If you get my voice mail, leave me a message and I'll call you back as soon as I can. I have a couple of shoots this week, but mostly some post work to do."

She nodded. "Okay. Thank you."

"Next Saturday," he said. "Six thirty. Text me your address so I know where I'm picking you up."

* * * *

The last thing Mallory wanted was her uncle starting shit in front of Kel. "You can just pick me up here," she quickly said.

His head tipped to the side. "I don't mind picking you up at your place."

That was when she realized how it might have sounded. "Sorry," she said. "My uncle…I really don't want a battle with him. I mean, if you want to pick me up there, okay, but I'll warn you in advance he might start something."

Something flashed in Kel's gaze, a brief, dark flare that disappeared as quickly as it had emerged. He stepped closer, capturing her hands again, gently squeezing. "Mal," he said, his tone lower, deeper. "If he gives you *any* trouble, I don't care what time of day or night it is, you *will* call me. Promise me."

She swallowed hard but nodded.

"Say it."

"I promise."

He smiled, resting his forehead against hers, still not releasing her hands. "As soon as Chelbie lets you have your phone back, text me your address so I know I have it. I'll pick you up at six thirty Saturday evening. And, if you want, I have a spare bedroom at my apartment. If you'd like to bring an overnight bag and spend the night at my place, you're more than welcomed to do that, too."

"I don't want to be an imposition." Inside, her heart screamed *yes, yes, yes!*

"I don't offer things if I feel it's going to be an imposition," he said. His voice dropped in volume, nearly to a whisper. "If you want to be my play partner, you will have to learn to take me at my word and not question my motives. I'm a grown-up. If I want to offer to do something, all you need to do is say yes or no. You don't need to try to figure out anything else beyond that. Can you do that?"

The dry *click* in her throat when she swallowed didn't go away when she swallowed a second time. "Yes," she whispered after summoning the courage to utter it.

Play partner?

Her knees felt weak.

A teasing smile curved his lips. "For the record," he added, "while I might rig other people, I don't have anyone else I consider a play partner."

"Me?" She wasn't aware she'd said it aloud until he moved in closer.

"You," he whispered. He placed another tender, scorching kiss on her forehead. Her eyes dropped closed, a soft whine escaping her.

"We can talk more during the week and next weekend," he said, giving her hands one final squeeze before releasing them and stepping back. "But the offer is on the table, if you want it. Now make sure to text me your address. I expect it on my phone before I get back to my place."

She nodded, heart racing.

He smiled. "Good night, Mal."

"Good night, Kel."

She stood there, watching him as he got back in his truck and pulled out of the driveway.

Play partners?

She nearly ran into the front door in her excitement to get inside and tell Chelbie. When she threw the door open, she ran smack into Chelbie, who'd been standing there eavesdropping.

"Well? I couldn't hear everything."

"I—" She remembered his admonishment. "I need my phone! I have to text him my address before he gets home!"

Chelbie spun on her heel and raced for her bedroom, Mallory close behind. With the bedroom door closed behind them, Mallory snatched her phone from Chelbie's hand, impatiently waited for it to power up, and quickly swiped through the text messages, missed call, and voice mail notifications—all from her uncle—that popped up.

After texting Kel her address, she looked up into Chelbie's expectant gaze.

"He said he wants us to be play partners. That he doesn't call anyone else a play partner."

Chelbie let out a piercing *squee* and engulfed Mallory in a crushing hug. "That's great! I *knew* he was into you!"

"That's not a relationship." She tried to control her excitement, tried to keep her brain in charge despite her heart's rebellion to the contrary.

"It's a damn good start," Chelbie countered. "Take him at his word. He's not trying to get you into bed right off the bat. He's taking things slow."

"He offered to let me stay at his place next Saturday night," she said. "After the club. He said he has a spare bedroom."

Chelbie's head cocked to the side. "Hmm. Let me think on that."

Mallory blinked. "Um, *my* decision."

Chelbie poked her in the chest. "Um, you're *my* bestie. I get veto powers if I think you're making a mistake. Just like you get veto powers over me. Let's see how this week goes."

"You said yourself you don't think he's dangerous."

"I said I don't think he's a killer. He earned massive brownie points for assuming I'd be part of the package last night and today. And next weekend," she added. "A predator usually likes to divide and conquer. Kel also doesn't have a player rep. But promise me, if I nix it, you'll listen to me. Right?"

Mallory loved Chelbie, knew her friend only had her best interests at heart. "Okay, fine."

Another crushing hug. "Now, what did Slimon have to say? I think I pissed him off last night."

"Ugh. I don't even know if I want to know." She stared at her phone's home screen. "I know I'll have a battle on my hands when I get home."

She remembered her promise to Kel.

Did he mean I could call him tonight?

She hoped he did.

Because if there was one thing she could count on, it was her uncle being a shithead.

Chapter Twelve

Mallory's stomach knotted into a painful ball of nerves as she slowly drove home. It was too tempting to flee somewhere else.

Anywhere else.

Preferably back into the safety and calm of Kel's arms, but she knew she had to face this like an adult.

When she pulled into the driveway, she was dismayed to see lights still on in the living room.

Dammit.

Taking a deep breath, she slowly got out, gathered her things from the car, and headed inside.

Saul didn't even let her get all the way inside the front door before he pounced on her, blocking her progress through the foyer. "Where the hell have you been? Why haven't you answered any of my texts or phone calls? And how dare that little bitch of a friend of yours talk to me like that!"

She lowered her head and started walking, forcing him to finally step aside or be plowed over. He harangued her all the way down the hall until, at her bedroom door, she whirled around.

"Stop it!" she screamed. "Just stop it! I told you I wouldn't be home until late tonight. How dare you harass me about this!"

He straightened. "It's time you stop hanging out with that girl. She's nothing but trouble."

"She's been more like family to me than *you've* ever been," she shot back as she walked in and dropped her stuff on the bed.

He stopped in the doorway. She didn't know if he rummaged through her room while she wasn't home or not. She'd never seen any evidence of him doing that, but ever since she'd turned eighteen, he'd stopped coming into her room even though he still vocalized his opinions of her housekeeping skills.

"Mallory Ann Weaver, you listen to me and you listen good. You *will* fill out that graduate school application and—"

She wheeled around and got in his face, rising up on her toes. "I want to see the fucking trust paperwork. Right now. Tonight. Go get it."

His eyes widened. "Quit trying to change the subject, young lady—"

"Stop with the 'young lady' crap. That worked on me when I was ten. It doesn't work on me anymore. The trust paperwork. Now."

He took a step back and crossed his arms over his chest. "I don't have to stand here and be insulted like this! I've taken care of you, took you in—"

"And I appreciate it. But it's time for me to take charge of my life. Go get them."

"The last thing you need right now is worrying about that. You have two more semesters of college, and then you'll go—"

"Out on my own. To work. The papers." Her heart pounded, her fists clenched. She knew, deep in her gut, that he wasn't going to show her the paperwork.

"You are going to quit that stupid job you have, focus on your studies, and focus on getting your master's degree."

She felt like she was stuck in a really bad *Twilight Zone* episode. "*Seriously?* Is there a name for your condition?" She pushed past him and headed down the hall toward the spare bedroom he used as his home office.

He managed to squeeze past her and stand in the doorway. "Just what do you think you're doing? Trying to deflect my attention from your atrocious behavior this weekend isn't going to work. I don't understand why you're fighting me about going to grad school. You will go, and that's final."

She laughed. Actually laughed in his face. "They're right. All of them. You're a fucking thief or something."

His face turned a shade of beet-red she'd never seen it take on before. "How *dare* you—"

"How dare *you*! I'm going to be twenty-three, Uncle Saul. I want to know what the hell's the deal with the trust. Obviously there's still money in it if you're so batshit crazy to get me into grad school. So fork it over."

"You have no clue how to manage a trust. I've been doing this for almost thirteen years now. If you think I'm going to let you squander away your future, you're sadly mistaken."

They had reached impasse. She didn't know what he'd do if she tried to get through that office door. Hell, if he had his desk or file cabinet locked, it wasn't like she could force the keys from him.

"And who was that man, hmm?" he said, startling her. "Oh, yes. I followed you and that little witch of a friend of yours this morning. I saw that man pick you up. And where was that he took you?"

"You *followed* me? You're *stalking* me now? What kind of sick freak are you?"

"What kind of sick freak are *you*?" he spat back. "I looked up that place you went today," he said. "Some sort of sex club. I'm sure the cops would love to hear about that. I can't believe it's still in business! Bet they'd love to hear from a concerned citizen about that, wouldn't they? And that guy, bet his photography clients would love to hear about the things he does in his spare time, huh?"

It was one thing for him to be a pain in her ass.

If Saul outed her friends or caused aggravation for the club, she'd never forgive herself for bringing that trouble down on top of them. At a loss to respond and too shocked to fight to discover what he'd done with the trust, she stormed back down the hall and slammed her bedroom door behind her, locking it.

On her bed, she saw her phone light up from an incoming text.

It was Kel.

Got it. :) Thank you for sending it.

Desperation set in. She didn't know what else to do. Chelbie's parents would likely already be asleep and wouldn't appreciate their world being upended over her family drama, no matter what they said to the contrary.

And Kel had been the one directly threatened by her uncle. She'd never known Saul to be so vindictive and ruthless. Whatever was going on, she knew she couldn't handle this on her own any longer.

She made the call.

Kel sounded concerned when he answered. "Mal? Everything okay?"

"No." She tried to hold back her tears as she quietly told him what had happened, the threats her uncle had made, everything spilling out of her.

All the while, feeling beyond terrified that Kel would be pissed off that she'd brought this down upon him and the club. And if he was, she wouldn't blame him in the least for it.

"Shh, okay, Mal," he said. "It's all right. Calm down. For starters, the club has all its paperwork and permits and is completely legal. So he's full of shit. Secondly, my clients can all see my portfolios. I make no secret of what I do in my free time, so he's full of shit there, too. Is he threatening you? Did he lay a hand on you?"

She jumped as Saul pounded on her door and she heard him try the doorknob.

"Mallory!" he yelled through the door. "I'm *not* kidding. Either you come out of there and agree to grad school, or I will put your friends through a world of public shame and make sure they know you could have stopped it!"

"Oh, will he?" Kel darkly said on the phone.

"You heard that?"

"Yes, I heard it. Sit tight."

"If you show up, I don't know what he'll do."

"Honey, listen to me." Kel dropped into that same tone he'd used on her when he told her to text him her address. "Someone's going to show up at your house in about twenty minutes or so. I won't be far behind them, but I have some calls to make first."

"Who?"

"Don't worry about it. You'll know them. Just let them in and let them deal with your uncle. You start packing whatever you need to get out of there. When I get there, we'll grab as much as we can, but if there's anything irreplaceable you need to take now, in case we can't get it all, make sure to have it ready."

"What?"

"You're moving in here for now. At least until we can get this sorted out for you and find out what the hell he's hiding. Understand me?"

"Yes, Sir." It slipped from her before she could stop it.

"Good girl," he said.

Her innards fluttered in a good way, until she jumped when her uncle pounded on her door again, yelling at her.

"Ignore him. If he puts a hand on you, call 911, and then call me back. Otherwise, I'll see you shortly. Keep your phone on you, in your pocket."

"Yes, Sir."

She ended the call and put the phone on the bed. Changing into shorts, she slid the phone into her back pocket as Kel had instructed before yelling at her uncle. "Go away. I'm not talking to you tonight."

"I'll be the only one talking to you when I finish with your friends—"

She yanked the door open and glared at him. "Then fucking *do* it," she said. "You're a nutless asshole, is what you are. I don't think you have the sac to do it. You're just fucking scared shitless that I'm going to find out whatever it is you're doing with the trust. It's funny how every time I mention the trust, you change the subject. What are *you* hiding, huh?"

Impasse. Again.

He glared at her, breathing heavy, staring at her, finally blinking first and turning to storm to his own bedroom, where he slammed the door behind him.

The shakes hit her again. She leaned against the doorway, struggling not to burst into tears.

Then, Kel's orders hit home, driving back into her conscious.

She ran out to the garage and grabbed a few empty boxes that had been stored out there, a couple of rolls of paper towels, and a box of garbage bags. Running back to her room, she locked the door behind her and quickly started packing her dragons. Some of them had been presents from her parents. She would hate to lose any of her books, but the dragons were irreplaceable.

She also had her photo albums in her room, and they went into another box. She dragged her boxes of dragons out of her closet, stacking everything next to her bed before she started emptying her dresser and closet into the garbage bags.

About eighteen minutes after her call to Kel, someone rang the front doorbell, then immediately pounded on the door before ringing the doorbell again.

Mallory ran out to the living room, hearing her uncle's bedroom door open behind her. Without looking to see who it was, she threw the front door open to find Tilly standing there. The older woman's gaze swept the room and she didn't even wait for Mal to invite her in as she walked right past her.

"You all right, Mal?" Tilly asked as she focused on Mallory's uncle now charging down the hallway toward them.

Heat shimmers of rage seemed to wash off the woman. Slender, and shorter than her uncle, Mal still had no doubts Tilly could hold her own against the man.

She'd seen Tilly scene at the club, both as a viciously sadistic Domme, and as a bottom to Landry and Cris.

Her uncle stormed into the living room. "Who the hell are you?"

Mallory pushed the front door closed as Tilly put on a chilling smile and walked over to him, extending her hand to shake with him. "Hi there. Tilly Cardinal. I'm a friend of Mallory's. I'm here to help her." Her cold tone would have frightened the crap out of Mal had it been focused on her.

Her uncle sounded dumbstruck. "Get the hell out of this house before I call the cops!"

"Oh?" Tilly's eyebrows dangerously arched as her smile faded. "Then I suppose when they get here I should tell them how I saw you shove Mallory against the wall and you threatened to kill her, hmm?"

When Mallory started to say something, Tilly held out a staying hand to her without taking her gaze off Saul.

"What?" he thundered.

"Why, yes. A friend of ours was on the phone with Mallory and heard you threatening her through the bedroom door. Of course, when I was called, since I'm so close, I rushed over just in time to witness you attacking her."

Tilly calmly stepped forward, her face inches from Saul's. "You're lucky I don't have a concealed carry license, asshole. That, and I don't feel like going to jail for premeditated homicide over someone as worthless as you."

She snapped her fingers at Mallory. "Keep packing your stuff while your uncle and I have a little chat. The others will be here any minute."

"Others?" her uncle yelled.

Tilly snapped her fingers in his face before pointing at him. "I wasn't talking to *you*, asshole. You will only talk when I tell you you can."

Mallory ran to follow Tilly's orders. She wasn't afraid of Tilly…

Okay, screw that, anyone in their right mind would be afraid of Tilly when she was in full-on Domme mode. But for tonight, at least, Tilly was on her side, and Mallory would be eternally grateful to the woman for it.

Tilly had subtly turned, forcing her uncle to turn and back toward the living room. "Now then," Mallory heard Tilly say before she headed down the hallway, "you are going to sit your damn ass down on that sofa, keep your mouth shut, or I *will* call the cops and there *will* be about six other witnesses here by the time they get here, all of them swearing that you threatened to kill her, and me for helping her. Including an FDLE officer and a detective from the Charlotte County Sheriff's Office. Try me if you think I'm kidding, you goddamned cunt nugget."

Holy shit.

Mallory felt glad these people were her friends and not her enemies!

When the doorbell rang a few minutes later, Tilly called out to her. "I've got it, Mal. I'll send them back. Don't stop what you're doing."

She heard several male voices enter the house. Then she turned.

Kel stood in her bedroom doorway.

That's when her emotional dam burst. With him there, she couldn't be strong anymore, no matter how much she hated herself for it. She started sobbing as he raced in, Seth, Cris, and Tony on his heels.

Kel engulfed her in his arms. "Shh," he said. "We got this. We're here. You're okay."

"Where do we start?" Seth asked him.

She thought she heard another familiar male voice, maybe Landry, out in the living room.

Kel looked around. "Grab anything already boxed or bagged up." He cradled her face in his hands. "Did he hurt you?"

She shook her head, unable to stop crying long enough to speak.

He pulled her close again. "Okay, sweetie. All right." He kissed the top of her head, stroked her hair, her back. "We got this for you. Ross will be here with some boxes in a couple of minutes, and we've got Josh, Ted, and Mark on the way with their trucks and more boxes, too. Where's your purse and laptop and stuff?"

She pointed at the bed.

He scooped her purse and laptop case off the bed and onto his shoulder before slipping an arm around her waist and leading her down the hallway and out the front door.

"Where are your keys?"

She fished them out of the side pocket of her purse, and only then did she realize there were now three other vehicles besides Kel's truck parked in her driveway and on the street in front of the house.

He unlocked her car for her, ushered her around to the passenger seat, and then reached across her and started it, turning on the AC.

"Lock yourself in," he said. "Do you have any medicine or anything you need out of the kitchen?"

"No. Just my stuff in the hall bathroom."

"We'll get that. Garage? Rest of the house?"

She thought about it. "The china cabinets, but don't worry about those. It's okay. Mainly the stuff in my room."

He leaned in and kissed her forehead. "Do *not* unlock this car unless it's one of us. You stay *here*. Okay? Do *not* move."

She nodded.

He closed the door and waited until he heard her hit the lock button before returning to the house.

She sat there, stunned and in shock as more people she recognized from the club arrived, including the three Collins brothers. Something akin to a well-organized military operation took place. Through the front windows, she watched Tilly and Landry standing over her uncle, who sat on the couch with an evil glare on his face and his arms crossed over his chest as he stared up at them. Meanwhile, the other men carried her things out, even her bookcase, dresser, and bed, and loaded them into various vehicles.

Less than thirty minutes later, it was done. Kel handed his keys off to Cris, who took off in Kel's truck, apparently leading the caravan.

Kel walked back to Mallory's car and tapped on the driver's side window. She unlocked the door. He opened it and smoothly slid into the driver's seat.

Her uncle appeared on the front porch.

Kel paused, waiting, arms resting on the steering wheel, staring at the other man until he finally went inside and slammed the front door shut.

Only then did Kel lean in and kiss her forehead. "Let's go home and get you unpacked."

Chapter Thirteen

Kel handed Mallory off to Tilly when they reached his apartment, ordering Mallory to stay on the couch while the men first removed the bed in the guest room before bringing her furniture and other belongings upstairs.

Tilly sat with one arm draped comfortingly around Mallory's shoulders as Mallory glanced at her phone.

"Do you want to call Chelbie tonight?" Tilly asked her.

"I should." It felt like she'd stumbled into an alternate dimension. In the space of just a couple of hours, her life had forever flipped on its axis.

Whether or not it would shake out to be a good thing remained to be seen.

"I'll do it for you, if you'd like."

Mallory unlocked her phone. "No, I'll do it." She hoped her friend's phone didn't wake up her parents.

When Chelbie answered, sounding a little sleepy, Mallory felt guilty for waking her up.

"What's wrong?" Chelbie asked, sounding more awake when she realized it was Mallory. "What'd that fucker Slimon do now?"

Mallory tried to tell her, but thinking about how her friends had swooped into protect and move her overwhelmed her again. Tilly gently took the phone from her.

"Hey, Chelbie? Sweetie, it's Tilly." Tilly gave her the condensed version of the story, then listened. "No, he didn't actually hurt her, but I think by the time Landry and I got done with him, he needed a change of shorts… Yes, we'll be here at Kel's for a while yet. Come on over. See you shortly."

She returned the phone. "Done." Tilly hugged her close. "Sweetie, don't you realize you're family to us?"

"Some of these guys barely know me."

"Yeah, but I know you well enough to call you family. And Kel apparently thinks an awful lot of you. As far as I'm concerned, that's good enough for me." She brushed Mallory's hair away from her face. "When we adopt someone, that's it. We don't let people fuck with our family."

"He threatened to out Kel and cause trouble for the club."

"Yeah? So? Kel's out. Not like he's a school teacher or something who has to worry about that. And the club, well, Derrick has all his shit in order, trust me. You don't need to worry about the club."

"I'm sorry I've dragged everyone into my drama. I never wanted to do that."

"I really wish you'd confided in me sooner," Tilly gently said. "If you had, we would have helped you get out of there long before now. I feel bad you've been going through this alone."

"I didn't want to bother anyone."

"You're not bothering anyone. Stop it. We want to help you. Let us."

"Now I don't know what to do about finding out about the trust."

"You leave that to us. Seth's going to handle getting the lawyer for you."

"I can't afford that."

"*Stop*. Oh, my god. You don't have to afford it. It's going to be done, and that's it. End of subject. If on the other side we find out you can afford it, he'll work with you then on his fee." Tilly gently shook her. "Until then, shut up and let your family take care of you."

A laugh finally escaped Mallory. "Yes, ma'am."

"That's more like it."

* * * *

Only being busy getting Mal's stuff moved into his apartment had kept Kel focused on not wanting to go back and beat the ever-lovin' snot out of her uncle.

When Chelbie arrived, dressed in a T-shirt and Eeyore PJ pants, she stormed barefoot up the stairs, her car keys in hand and hair a mess, practically throwing herself onto Mallory.

"Oh, my god. Are you okay?"

Tilly slid over to make room on the couch for Chelbie on Mal's other side. Kel walked in to join them, sitting on the coffee table in front of them.

"I'm okay," Mal sniffled.

"Why didn't you call me, girlie?" Chelbie asked.

Kel took over telling Chelbie as much of the story as he knew it. He suspected once Mal calmed down enough to retell everything, it would enrage him all over again when he heard any details she'd left out of their initial phone call.

Chelbie looked ready to kill. "I know that fucker's up to no fucking good. Fucker. Fucking fuckhead."

"Tell us how you really feel," Tilly snarked.

Chelbie reached over and grabbed Tilly's hand, squeezing. "Thank you for being there for her."

"Hey, like I already told her, she's family. And so are you. We take care of family."

"I know my parents will let her move in with us if she needs to," Chelbie said. She looked at Kel, and he caught the hint of warning, both in her narrowed gaze and dark tone. "I know this wasn't in your plans. We can move her to my house once I talk to my parents tomorrow."

He didn't want to piss Chelbie off, or come off sounding controlling, but he also knew he didn't want Mal to move out. If nothing else, he wanted her there, safe with him, able to protect her if her uncle tried anything.

"She's welcomed to live with me as long as she wants or needs to," he said. "Once things calm down, we'll discuss rent and stuff. But seriously, it's all right."

Chelbie looked from him to Mal and back again. "No offense, dude, but I'm going to be the voice of reason here." She focused on Mallory again. "You're upset and not thinking clearly right now. I'm beyond grateful he got you out of there and safe, but keep in mind that this is *not* your only option."

Tilly apparently cued into Chelbie's thoughts. "She's right. I know and trust Kel to be a stand-up guy, but he's been in the lifestyle long enough, he won't hold it against you if you decide you'd be more comfortable at Chelbie's house. And, believe me, no one will mind helping you move again. Seriously. It is not an imposition."

Mallory met his gaze. Kel nodded, wanting to assure her. "They're right. I wanted you safe. This was the first and easiest option. You are not obligated to me, but I really mean it when I say if you'd like to live here, I am happy to have you here for as long as you'd like. No expectations other than friends and roommates."

Mallory grabbed Chelbie and Tilly's hands. "Thank you. All of you. I think I'd like to try being here, at least at first." She looked at Chelbie. "I love you, but moving in with your parents, I'm afraid that would be like another crutch. If I'm here and forced to make my own way, maybe that will help me stay stronger and get through all this the way I need to."

"Okay, girlie. I understand." Chelbie hugged her, but shot Kel a warning glare he had no trouble interpreting.

They'll never find your body.

Tilly joined in their hug and also met his gaze. Her dark stare was softened only by her wink, which he also could interpret.

I'll help Chelbie hide your body.

He leaned in and wrapped his arms around all three women. "If any of you think I'd do anything to risk incurring the wrath of either of these two, think again. I value my boy parts too much to be an idiot."

Mallory laughed, lightening his soul with the sound. As Tilly and Chelbie released her, she leaned in and hugged him, snuggling against him.

"Thank you," she said. "I do trust you. You have no idea how much I appreciate all you've done for me tonight. I'm overwhelmed."

"I know." He reluctantly released her. "That's why we're not going to discuss the finances for a little while yet. We're going to get you an appointment with the attorney, get that ball rolling, and let you decompress for a while."

So much for me not inviting drama llamas into my corral.

No, that wasn't fair. This wasn't Mallory's fault. It wasn't like she'd tried to stir up trouble. She was only guilty of being young and trusting and letting her uncle boss her around. Easy trap to fall into, considering the circumstances. He wouldn't hold that against her.

Especially when all he wanted to hold against her was his own body.

* * * *

Seth, Tony, Chelbie, and Tilly hung back after everyone had finished unloading her things. Much of her stuff, boxes and bags of clothes, lined the hallway leading to the bedroom that was now hers. Seth hung back in the living room, talking on the phone with someone, while Mallory and the others walked down to the bedroom.

Mallory was blown away to see that they had arranged the furniture as best they could to approximate her other room. She also now had an extra dresser and two more bookcases. Fortunately, the bedroom was a little larger than her old one.

One box, labeled *WALLS* in an unfamiliar hand, sat on the other dresser. "I don't know if you had a specific order or something," Kel apologized. "I took pictures with my phone before I pulled everything down."

She walked over and opened it. Inside lay all the papers she'd had hanging on her walls from the other house.

Turning, she hugged him. "Thank you," she said. "I didn't even think about those." She had pictures and in some cases electronic versions, or scans, of her works, but it was nice to know all of them had made the move with her.

"And if you want to paint in here, we can do that, too. Make it yours for as long as you're here."

"I'm sorry it looked like such a mess. I wasn't really allowed to spread out around the house."

"Stop apologizing," he said, a playful smile filling his features. "Or I'll spank you."

"Oooh," Chelbie said. "Apologize again. Pleeease?"

"Some friend you are."

Tilly hummed "The Wheels on the Bus" song, making them all laugh.

Seth ended his phone call and joined them, talking to them from the bedroom doorway. "Okay. Tomorrow, nine o'clock. Leah and I will come pick you up and take you to see Ed."

"Ed?"

"The attorney. You, too, Kel," he added. "If you want."

"I want."

Tilly hugged her. "Then that's settled. It's been a long, long night. You try to get some rest. What's your phone number?" Mallory told her, and Tilly punched it into her phone, then sent a text.

Mallory's phone vibrated in her back pocket. "There you go," Tilly said. "Text or call me if you need me, or need to talk. Day or night. If Uncle Douchecanoe gives you any trouble, you tell me immediately."

"Tilly," Seth playfully said, "we don't want to have to bail you out of jail. Let's see what Ed digs up."

"I'm just sayin'."

Chelbie nodded. "Yeah. I'm with her. We can alibi each other."

The women nodded, and Mallory knew they were on their way to becoming close friends, too.

Once everyone had left and it was just Kel and Mallory alone, he gave her one last hug. "Seriously, don't worry about unpacking tonight. Just get what you need for tomorrow. We'll deal with this later. It's not going anywhere. Nine o'clock is going to come really early in the morning.

Her brain spun. "I still can't believe all this happened."

"Believe it. We'll get you through the legal stuff, get that straightened out for you, and then from there you can decide what you want to do."

"I hope he doesn't cut off my funding for school. I still have two more semesters."

"We'll deal with that if it happens." He rested his hands on her shoulders and she realized that was quickly becoming one of her favorite things. It felt comforting, like he was in complete control, ready and willing to take charge, not steamroll over her. "Tonight, get some sleep. Okay?"

She nodded. "Yes, Sir."

A bright smile lit his face. "You don't have to call me that if you don't want to, but I don't mind."

"Good. I don't mind, either."

He softly closed the bedroom door behind him, and she heard him walk downstairs, presumably to check the locks on the office door and the large, roll-up door in front of the bay space.

She sank onto the bed and looked around, feeling caught in an emotional time-warp. Remembering how it felt settling into her new room in the old house when she moved to Florida, how some of her furniture had made the move, while some hadn't, sold off by her uncle in an estate sale. Her aunt had stood up for her and made sure any toys or books she wanted were brought, but there were a couple of things, like a bookcase, that she'd wanted to bring that her uncle nixed with the rationale that they could easily buy another one once she was in Florida.

And things like her father's chair, the one he'd sat in every night after getting home from work, the one that smelled like him, that she'd curled up in and cried when the police told her that her parents were dead.

She'd never forgive her uncle for not letting her bring that chair.

Never again. Now, she was impossibly out from under his thumb physically.

All she had to do was let her newly adopted family lead her through the process of unraveling the financial and legal entanglements that he still lorded over her head.

And once she was done with him…

Well, he could go piss up a rope as far as she was concerned. He hadn't earned the right to be her family. Not after the way he'd acted.

She only hoped once they figured out what secrets he was hiding that she would still be able to finish school and get her degree.

We'll deal with that if it happens. She could even replay Kel saying it to her, in his comforting tone.

For the first time since her parents died, she finally felt like she had a family again.

Chapter Fourteen

Kel and Mallory were waiting when Seth called to let them know they were parked downstairs. Mallory swallowed back her nerves when she saw Kel dressed in a charcoal suit, light blue dress shirt, navy tie, and dress shoes.

He smiled. "You look surprised."

"I…you clean up well."

Stupid!

He grinned. "I don't put on a suit for just anyone, you know. Only the people I care deeply about." He held his arm out, indicating for her to go first down the stairs. When they reached the office, he opened the front door for her and held it. "I have to set the alarm. Hold on."

She got into the backseat of Seth and Leah's car. Both of them turned, offering her kind smiles. "Ready?"

"No," she admitted, "but this has to be done. I'm scared what they'll find out."

"Ed's good, and he's a bulldog. Don't worry. If there's a way to untangle this mess, he'll find it."

Kel joined her in the backseat, and she was glad when he reached over and held her hand after they'd buckled their seat belts. She was even more glad when he, as well as Seth and Leah, joined her in Ed's office.

It brought back too many bad, sad, painful memories. Lawyers and death. Being pulled from everything she knew and sent to Florida.

Taking a deep breath, she shoved those thoughts out of her mind and tried to focus on the attorney.

He offered her a friendly smile. "For starters, Seth told me some of the things your uncle said last night. Rest assured, nothing about your personal life will shock me. Let's put that fear to rest right now. Secondly, your uncle can threaten all he wants, but I have no problem offering my services for free to anyone he does out, and keeping him tied up in a nightmare of legal limbo for the next twenty years. Understand?"

She nodded.

He had her start with her personal information, getting copies of her driver's license, social security card, and birth certificate, all things she had with her. Her parents' information, as well as her father's military service records, were in her uncle's office with the other paperwork.

He walked her through as much as she could remember, places, names, dates, including her grandfather's information in New Jersey. By the time they finished nearly an hour later, he looked thoughtful.

"I'm going to get started digging up what I can. Meanwhile, I will send a certified letter to your uncle, demanding he immediately turn over all records about the trust and any and all bank accounts. If he refuses, the next step is we take him to court."

"I can already tell you he'll refuse."

"Maybe. But I have steps to take legally before we can proceed. Meanwhile, I'll see what I can dig up in Rapid City and in New Jersey regarding probate on the estates of your parents and your grandfather. It's all public record."

"Thank you."

He took off his glasses and peered at her across his desk. "I know this is all scary. I understand that. But these people are my friends, and I'll tell you what I've already told them. We won't worry about any costs or fees until we get through the other side of this. If there isn't any money, we'll figure it out. If we find there is something there, we'll discuss a fee after we're done. I might be able to sock your uncle for all the legal fees and court costs, depending on what we find. So please don't worry about that."

"I appreciate it."

He stood. "It'll probably take a couple of weeks, or longer. I'll keep in touch with you and let you know what the next step is once I get done with my research and contact your uncle. So try to go about your life, try to settle in, try not to worry."

When they were in the car and on the way back to Kel's apartment, he said, "Can we stop by Dom Depot? I need to get extra keys made for her."

Seth laughed. "My favorite store? Are you kidding? Of course." It was a common nickname among lifestylers for the home improvement store chain.

Leah giggled and looked over her shoulder at Mallory. "Oh, boy. We're in trouble."

"*You* might be in trouble," Seth said. "Mallory's only in trouble if she wants to be."

She blushed, glancing at Kel before facing forward again. "Only if it's the good kind of trouble," she finally said.

The other three laughed. "Mal," Seth said, "you realize we only tease the people we love, right?"

"I'm getting that. I'd hate to see what you do to the people you don't like."

"We sic Tilly on them," the three of them said in unison before bursting into laughter.

* * * *

When they returned to the apartment, Kel showed her how to set and turn off the alarm. He'd forgotten to set it when he'd raced out the night before, which worked out in the end, since he'd been able to hand his keys off for the others to get started.

He also checked to make sure the keys to the knob and deadbolt, as well as the padlocks on the large, roll-up door worked.

He handed them over to her. "There you go, Mal. Home sweet home."

She seemed to weigh them in her palm. "Thank you. I guess I need to get a spare made for my car. I left them in the kitchen drawer. I didn't even think about that."

"No worries. We'll get that done. Why don't you start unpacking? No rush on getting it done today. Do you need to go in to work?"

"Oh, yeah." She winced. "I totally forgot about that. I'm sorry. I'll try to get everything out of the hallway tonight."

"Mal, seriously." He rested his hands on her shoulders. He noticed she always seemed to relax when he did it. "I mean it. Take your time. I mean, sure, if they're still in the hall in three weeks I might say something, but if it takes you a few days, I'm good with that."

"I can't begin to tell you how much I appreciate all of this. All of you. What you all did for me..." She let out a sad sigh he felt to his very depths.

He tucked a loose hair behind her ear. "You're family. It's what we do."

Speaking of family, he waited until after Mallory had left for her job to call his mom. He'd meant to do it Sunday afternoon, but then got busy with Mallory and Chelbie, and then...

His world had exploded in the good kind of way.

She answered on the third ring. "Hey, you."

"Hi, Mom." He settled into his chair behind his desk and booted up his large desktop computer. "How you doing?"

"I got the fire ants."

He laughed. "Good for you." His mom had been in a war against them in her yard for weeks.

"Didn't need the poison, either..."

And there she went, off on her diatribe about how she managed to overcome her tiny demon insect foes without the use of pesticides.

She was devoted to her two miniature Dachshunds and had refused to use anything that might accidentally hurt them.

"So what's new with you?" she asked.

He hesitated. He didn't know what to say, other than to state the bare-bones facts. "I've got a roommate. At least for a while."

"Oh, really?"

"Yeah." He told her, leaving out that he'd met her through the club. He used the common euphemism of "mutual friends," and talked about them all going out to eat, getting together again, and then the late-night distress call.

When he finished, his mom didn't respond at first.

"Mom?"

"I'm here."

"Why do you not sound happy?"

"It's not that I'm unhappy. I just want you to be careful."

"I am."

"She's, what, nine years younger than you? Alone in the world? Make sure your other friends are pulling their weight, too, so she's not leaning just on you."

This coming from the woman who refuses to date. "I know, Mom. I'm not a kid."

"I didn't say you were. So can you two come over for dinner on Friday?"

He thought about it. His first inclination was to say no, afraid that might overwhelm Mal.

"I'll have to ask her if her work schedule will allow it, but let's say a tentative yes."

"Find out if she's got any food allergies and call me tomorrow."

"Will do."

"Love you, Kelly."

He smiled. His mom was the only one who ever called him that. To everyone else, he was either Askel, or Kel. "Love you, too, Mom."

* * * *

That night, after Mallory got home from work, Kel asked her about going to eat at his mom's with him. She looked reluctant at first.

"I promise, we'll just go as friends."

"How do we explain how we met?"

"I already did. We have 'mutual friends.'"

"Oh. Okay."

He stood in the doorway of her room. "Also, I want to lay down some ground rules for us."

He watched the caution enter her body language, her expression. "All right."

"Nothing complicated. But this is my home. I ask that if you're going to bring anyone here, you ask me first."

"What about Chelbie?"

"Okay, clarification. Chelbie, or any of our friends from the club that we're mutual friends with, that's different." He took the plunge. "But you don't bring back any…dates, even if I know them, without asking me first."

He thought she might balk at that, but to his pleasant surprise, she nodded. "Not a problem. Not like I'm going to be dating anyway."

He couldn't decipher her tone, if it was meant to be self-deprecating or not. So he added a little disclaimer. "That's a two-way street. I won't be bringing anyone back here, either."

She seemed to be studying him.

"We're play partners, right?" he asked.

She nodded.

"Okay, then. We're also friends. Aren't we?"

She nodded a little harder.

"Good. Let's leave things like this for now, then. We're friends and play partners living together. You just went through a lot of stuff. We have to get you through whatever legal proceedings have to happen. For now, our lives are simplified by limiting our…intimate circle to only each other. And by intimate, I mean we agree that if we do decide we want to go out with someone, we clear it with the other person first. I'm not looking for a girlfriend, and let's be honest, you don't need a boyfriend to complicate your situation until you're steady on your feet. Agreed?"

This time, he didn't miss how she quickly seemed to blink away tears as she nodded.

Somehow, he felt like maybe he'd made things a little worse instead of better, but was at a loss to fix it. Deciding to quit while he was ahead, he said good night and headed to his room.

* * * *

Mal sat there, the half-emptied box in front of her, and tried to figure out what the hell that had meant. Okay, so he wouldn't be dating. Great.

Wasn't like she'd be dating. If she was to date anyone, it'd be Kel.

Did that mean he liked her? Or that he didn't want anyone else being with her? Was it a potential future, or simply a practical arrangement to prevent feelings from getting hurt?

And he's taking me to meet his mother?

She sat back and tried to figure it out.

Maybe I don't want *to figure it out.*

Especially if he'd meant it more in the sparing her feelings kind of way.

Shoving those thoughts aside, she went back to unpacking. She wanted to get her room tidied so he didn't think she was a slob.

She'd even taken the time to make her bed that morning.

Chapter Fifteen

Mallory flinched when she heard Kel slam something onto his desk in his office downstairs. "Dammit," he grumbled, just loudly enough she could hear him.

In the nearly four weeks they'd lived together, even though they'd grown to be very close friends, she still was trying to get used to some of Kel's moods. When he got aggravated, he never directed it at her, like her uncle had, but her old ingrained reactions were sometimes hard to overcome.

That wasn't Kel's fault. She knew that. It was something she'd have to get over and past on her own. This wasn't her home. It was his, even though in the short amount of time she'd lived with him it felt more like any home she'd had since her parents' deaths.

Ed had called her last week to update her. To let her know that her uncle had failed to respond to the certified letter, and that Ed had people working on digging up information. He also told her while he didn't want to get her hopes up too soon, that the initial information he'd discovered looked promising, but he'd rather wait to tell her about it until he knew for sure.

Other than her own nerves, she and Kel had settled into a very comfortable routine, sharing chores and spending time together when not working. She never felt pressured by him in any way, and he never made any advances toward her.

Although she was starting to wish he would.

To her shock, her uncle hadn't tried to contact her again, but her weekly stipend had still appeared in her bank account the past four weeks. She didn't know how long that would last, but she was being very careful with that money, as well as her paychecks from working at the consignment shop. Kel had set her initial rent and utilities at only one hundred a month for the first three months, to be renegotiated after that. She was responsible for chipping in for groceries, but since they'd started shopping together, that had been easy to do.

She made her bed every day, too, not wanting him to think she was a slob or anything.

Fighting the urge to lock her bedroom door and cower in bed, she forced herself out into the hallway and downstairs to the office. She found Kel leaning back in his chair, his chin propped up in the palm of one hand, elbow on the chair's arm.

Storm clouds darkened his normally placid face.

"What's wrong?" she dared ask.

When she spoke, the darkness fled his features as he offered her an apologetic smile. "Sorry. I didn't mean to startle you. Stupid model just flaked out on me. That is the last time I will ever use her. She flaked out on me once before, but I gave her a pass because she gave me a good song and dance over it."

"Oh." She leaned against the doorway, arms crossed over her chest. "Model for what?"

"That suspension gig I'm shooting next door this evening. I've got a top rigger wanting my byline on his shots, and no damn model for him to rig. This is *not* going to look good. I don't have anyone else I can call on such short notice."

Mallory's breath hitched in her throat as she caught and swallowed back the words she'd been about to say. Instead, she asked, "Who is it? The rigger, I mean." She remembered Kel telling her about the shoot, but honestly hadn't heard who the rigger was.

"Jaymzon Jordan."

She gasped. "Oh, damn." Even she knew who he was. One of the best-known riggers in the world, he'd starred in bondage films and had a bustling website selling photos and video clips. He was an innovator in the world of bondage and suspension. Every serious professional bondage model wanted to be tied by him and photographed for their portfolios, and every rigger attempted to imitate his intricate and artistic ties, as well as his nontraditional bondage techniques.

Kel swiveled his chair so he could look at her, dropping his hands into his lap. "Yeah." Dejection swirled, replacing the storm clouds. "I've been looking forward to working with him. I blow this, I'll likely never get another chance with him. He's a perfectionist. He was in Naples for another shoot, and called me to see if I wanted to work with him on this."

"Can you get anyone else to fill in? Any other models?"

"No one that I trust in just a couple of hours, who could do the work required of them. Tony and Shayla are out of town until tomorrow, but I doubt Tony would let her get rigged by him, anyway. He doesn't let anyone tie Shayla unless he knows them personally. There's no way Laura and Rob could get up here on such short notice. And I've heard Seth's opinions on Jaymzon enough to know he'd laugh right in my face if I asked if Leah could be tied by him. That's if he didn't tell me to go fuck myself first. Not worth losing my friendship with them over the gig."

"Why would Seth do that?" She couldn't imagine the friendly man getting that upset.

Kel stretched his arms over his head, his spine audibly popping even from across the office. "Seth saw Jaymzon get into an online sparring match with some jackass on FetLife a couple of years ago. Jaymzon came off looking like a raging douchenozzle in the process, even though he was, technically, in the right. Seth doesn't suffer douchenozzles lightly, regardless of how right they are."

Her swallowed words regurgitated, even though her anticipation of being shot down nearly nauseated her. "I could do it," she softly said. Heat filled her face, her gaze dropping to the floor as she hugged herself more tightly.

It would come any second, the laughter, the rejection. Then again, in the four weeks she'd lived there, he'd never, not once, made fun of her or teased her in anything but a loving and playful way.

Wait for it...

But he didn't respond. In fact, he didn't respond for so long that she finally had to look to see if he'd even heard her. Maybe she'd imagined saying it in the first place.

To her amazement, she found him studying her, his head slightly cocked, hands laced together and resting on top of his head.

"Really?" he finally asked.

She wasn't sure what context he meant that, curious or snarky.

And asking him to clarify wasn't in her. It'd taken every last ounce of courage she'd had to make the offer in the first place.

She nodded. "I mean," she quickly added, "I get it if I'm too fat. I know that a lot of the riggers are looking for—"

"*Stop*," he said.

His stern, harsh tone made her flinch again. He got up from his chair and walked over to her, tilting her chin up until she was forced to look him in those deep brown eyes.

"What did I tell you," he softly said, "about putting yourself down?"

Every last ounce of nerve in her struggled to keep her focus on him and not look down at her feet. "Don't do it."

"Right." He released her chin. "You're *not* fat. I don't care what the damn body charts say. You're beautiful, and you're healthy. That's all that matters. A number on a scale doesn't mean a damn thing if you can't be happy with what's inside you first. You'll never find happiness in a scale. Ever." He lightly rested his hands on her shoulders. "What's your height and weight?"

"Five six. I think I'm one sixty right now. I came down a pound after my period ended."

"Well, you're in luck. If you really mean it. But it's going to be a full-face, full-nude shoot. No masks or hoods. Is that something you're prepared to deal with?"

"Is it a sex shoot?"

"No. He's got a couple of new rigging techniques he wants photographed, and he needs the big space and the A-frame in Venture to do it. It'll be a long and tedious shoot."

"Needles?"

He smiled. "No. Just ropework. Well, bondage. He's using some stuff in addition to rope, which is why he needs the beefy A-frame. Just modeling. No play, no impact, nothing like that."

She swallowed and nodded, her heart stampeding in her chest. If she could do this, maybe Kel would see her as more than just a chaos-prone accident waiting to happen. Maybe he would see her the way she wished he'd see her.

"It's going to pay five hundred," Kel said, "but we'll be shooting for probably close to twelve hours. You up for that? No wussing out halfway through to say it's past your bedtime."

"I can do it."

"You're going to need some decent make-up." He glanced at his watch. "You've got three hours to go buy some, get a shower, and shave everything from the neck down. You have a black G-string?"

"I think so."

"If not, add it to your shopping list. Do you need any money? I can advance it against what you'll be paid."

Her face filled with heat again. "Yes, please." She *haaated* admitting that. She didn't know yet if her uncle would pay her tuition for the next semester or not. She needed to hoard absolutely every last penny she could in case he didn't.

Reaching into his pocket, Kel pulled out his wallet and thumbed through it. "Here's a hundred dollars." He handed her five twenties, but didn't let go of them when she reached for them. "I'm trusting you with this," he said. "And I don't just mean the money. I'm trusting you not to let me down."

"I won't. I promise."

"Don't promise me. Just carry through with it. Don't tell me. Show me."

"I will."

He released the money and turned to back to his desk. She hurried upstairs to her room, grabbed her purse, phone, and keys, and pounded down the stairs and out through the office door to her car.

No, I won't let you down. I promise.

No way would she blow this chance. Especially when she suspected if she did, it would be her only chance.

And he'd called her beautiful.

If for no other reason than that, she *damn* sure wouldn't let him down.

Chapter Sixteen

Kel dropped into his chair after she bolted from his office and headed upstairs. Moments later, she blew past him and out the front door, barely hesitating to lock it behind her. Then the faint sound of her car starting outside, and her driving away.

I hope this isn't a mistake.

He couldn't say he wasn't attracted to her. That would be a lie. He was.

But after his last dating experience with Krystal, he'd sworn he would not get involved with someone who didn't have their shit together.

And in his experience, that seemed to be a majority of the eligible dating pool in that area. Well, of women he found attractive.

He definitely found Mallory attractive. He wasn't lying when he'd called her beautiful. She was.

So what if she had extra curves on her body? She was still beautiful. A beautiful person, a beautiful personality, an amazing mind, and a gorgeous, sexy package to boot. Even if she didn't think she was. He'd seen the way men looked at her at Venture when they played. Likely there would be guys creeping out of the woodwork to hit on her if he and Tony and Tilly hadn't quietly put the word out that she was under their protection.

He just had to work on her self-esteem, because that still lay deep in the crapper.

He'd resisted using her as a model before because he didn't want her to cling to him, to get her hopes up that there might be a chance for more between them when he didn't know if there ever would be.

If it wasn't for the fact he knew he couldn't get another suitable model between now and when Jaymzon arrived, he wouldn't have agreed to this. He suspected she thought his refusals had been because he wasn't attracted to her. A faulty assumption on her part.

Attraction wasn't the issue. He had no difficulty imagining any number of positions he'd love to tie her in and fuck her silly, spend hours making her come, showing her what a beautiful woman he thought she was.

Marking her flesh in a way no one else had before.

Not my circus, not my monkeys.

She was his friend, yes. As much as he loved her, she did not have her act together yet. The fact that life circumstances beyond her control had put her in this position wasn't lost on him by any stretch of the imagination. Her uncle was a controlling asshole, sure. But she would have to find the inner strength to stand up to him and get her life on track. Twenty-two wasn't exactly a child. If she didn't make those realizations herself, she would spend her life being a victim without realizing it.

He had no interest in a victim. No interest in "fixing" someone. Life was hard, sucky, and frequently anything but fair. He'd had a couple of lucky breaks, but he'd had his share of bad ones, too.

She'd need a pair of bootstraps to yank herself up by if she didn't want to spend the rest of her life under her uncle's thumb.

And only she could do that. Everything she'd done thus far, in the short time he'd spent close to her, showed she appeared to be struggling to get her life on the right path. He would cheer her every inch of the way, help her if he could without enabling her, and support her as a friend.

Hopefully Ed would get her legal and financial mess straightened out and get her some answers so she could quit living in limbo.

Losing his heart to her until that happened and was all settled, however, wasn't something he'd allow. No matter how beautiful he thought she was.

Kel lost himself in his work while waiting for Mallory's return. Jaymzon wasn't a rigger tied to only one body type. And he was notorious for loving to work with newbie models, fresh faces, be the one to launch their careers. It fed into his slightly narcissistic desires for attention. The rigger had done shoots with plus-sized models before. And that he would be using his new techniques not only on a new model, but on a model many women would easily relate to, would be a massive ego boost for the guy.

For his part, Kel knew his only issue that night would be keeping his jealousy firmly in check. He'd heard plenty about Jaymzon's reputation in the rigging world. No, he was a professional while the lights were on and the cameras rolling, but after, it wasn't uncommon for him to flirt with the models, ask them out, or invite them back to his room.

Would Mallory remember the rules she'd agreed to in the heat of the evening and under the onslaught of Jaymzon's considerable charms, or would she disappoint Kel by eagerly going off with the rigger later?

Not that he had any say either way. He didn't have an official relationship with her beyond friends, play partners, and tenant and landlord.

I'm a fucking dumbass.

If he ended up losing her simply because he'd been too chickenshit to admit he was attracted to her, he'd never forgive himself.

He scrubbed his face with his hands, irritation stealing his focus. He was falling for her. *Had* fallen for her. He couldn't deny it.

But he refused to get dragged into some unhealthy dynamic that would turn his otherwise peaceful life upside down.

Been there, done that, got the farking T-shirt. So far, having Mal living with him had been a positive experience. She was easy to like, easy to live with, considerate, and fun to be around.

Time. That was all he could do was wait, give it time, and try not to get his hopes up unreasonably.

Because if he did, he'd have no one but himself to blame.

* * * *

Mallory sped to the mall and hit one of the cosmetics stores there for a free makeover. So as not to feel too guilty, she made some excuses and only bought a couple of the products they'd used—a foundation and blush—leaving her nearly sixty dollars. However, now armed with the knowledge of what she needed, she left there and headed straight to Target to load up on affordable eye shadow, lipstick, eyeliner, and other items in the colors the girl had told her would work well with her skin tone.

She also grabbed a black thong for only three dollars, and a blue satin bathrobe on clearance for eight.

It meant she wouldn't have to wear her worn, pink terrycloth robe to cover herself.

Making it back to the warehouse just a little over an hour later, she pounded up the stairs with her purchases and to her room, dumping everything on the bed.

She heard Kel follow her upstairs until he stood outside her door. "Everything okay?"

She turned, smiling. "Yeah." She pointed to her face. "How is this?"

* * * *

With only the little bit of makeup he'd seen her wear in the past, she'd been beautiful.

With the professionally applied makeup now artfully highlighting and accentuating her features, she looked stunning.

He nodded, swallowing hard. "Perfect. Gorgeous."

"Great! Now I need to get my shower." She turned back to the mirror. "I hope I can remember how she did it."

"Okay. Enjoy." He turned and hurried back to his office, tugging at the front of his shorts where his painfully throbbing erection strained against the fabric.

Holy...hell.

He didn't know if it was the makeup or her happy expression, but she'd transformed from a forty-watt bulb into a thousand-watt spotlight in terms of brilliance.

I can do this. I can be professional. I've worked with hundreds of bondage models over the years.

But none of them had been ones he'd felt such a visceral attraction to before. Then again, he hadn't had any kind of a personal relationship with other models beyond negotiating their shoot and salary before the sessions began.

It was going to be a *really* long night.

* * * *

Mallory fought off a sick wave of panic as she started reapplying the makeup after she finished styling her hair. She'd taken several selfies with her phone before her shower, hoping she could emulate the results the professional had achieved.

Okay, so she wasn't a dog. She'd admit that. Despite the extra pounds she carried, she was pretty.

It felt like a small weight rolled from her shoulders at that admission.

But am I pretty enough to hold Kel's attention?

Truth be told, he was the only one she felt an attraction toward. Yes, there were some nice-looking single guys at the club. A few had even made advances at her over the past couple of weeks, but the only man she had eyes for slept in the next room.

And he had as of yet to make an inappropriate move toward her despite the increasingly sexy banter they shared during their scenes.

He also didn't have a relationship. Sure, he played with others at the club, but she was satisfied to note he didn't spend a fraction of the time with them now that he did with her. And he only gave her aftercare. Whenever he took a break, he always sought her out, stayed by her side, frequently holding her hand or with his arm draped around her shoulders or waist.

A silent message of ownership.

Then there was the fact that whenever she played with anyone else, he'd always stepped in and briefly spoken with the Top before they got started. And while it was going on, he didn't play with anyone else, watching their scene until the end and he was satisfied she was safe, and providing her aftercare until she'd recovered.

It made her feel protected.

What she wanted to feel was desired. Kel always came right up to but not quite crossing the line of desire. Lust. Need.

He knocked on the bathroom doorway.

"Come in."

He opened the door. When she turned, satisfaction filled her to see his eyebrows lift. When she glanced down at his crotch, she didn't miss that he quickly adjusted himself.

Good.

* * * *

Holy…fuck.

If it hadn't been for the fact that they were about to start a job, he would have begged her to sit down with him right then, establish the rules of their relationship, and proceed to fuck her brains out.

No. Focus.

Fuck.

"Well?" she asked.

He nodded. "Wow. Good wow. Perfect."

She smiled. "Thank you."

He stared and then realized she was waiting for him to say something else. "Um, I'll drive you over there when it's time, so you don't have to walk all the way around the building in the heat."

Or so anyone can see how you look hotter than fuck like that.

He'd never been a jealous or possessive person.

Until now.

How the *hell* was he going to get through this shoot and remain professional?

He went next door to get the club ready, to get the AC turned on, the backdrop hung, and move his equipment over.

All the while, firmly in his brain sat the image of Mallory standing there in that gorgeous satin robe, her hair long and straight from using a flat-iron, falling over her shoulder in a brilliant, fiery cascade, and how he wished he could grab fistfuls of her hair and wrap it around his hands while she deep-throated his cock.

Oooh, stop that. This will be a long damn night if you can't get it under control.

He made sure he had water, snacks, and other supplies for her, and that she took her makeup, hairbrush, and a change of clothes for after. Then he drove her over, something in the back of his mind hoping Jaymzon would call and cancel at the last minute.

Kel would gladly pay her the rest of the money out of his own pocket.

When he heard the knock on the club's door, he walked out to the lobby, his heart sinking to see the rigger waiting outside. Six five and built like a brick shithouse, his shaved head and tanned skin glowed under the lights in the parking lot. Kel suspected the man must spend hours every day in the gym to look the way he did.

Schooling his expression, Kel unlocked the door and shook hands with him. "Hey, dude. Welcome to Sarasota."

"Glad we could work together," Jaymzon said. "Let me scope the setup before me and my guys bring our equipment in."

"Sure." He led him into the club.

"This is sweet. Nice to have your own—Well, *hello* there."

Something twisted, sick, deep in Kel's gut as Jaymzon walked over to where Mal sat waiting on one of the sofas.

The rigger didn't bother looking at Kel when he spoke. "I take it this lovely young lady is my victim, eh, model tonight?" He chuckled, drawing a nervous smile from Mal.

Kel wanted to deck him. The guy was in his early fifties. Not that age differences were usually a problem for Kel, but…

Well, okay, *any* guy who oozed this level of attraction toward Mal would set off Kel's alarms, regardless of whether he was eighteen or eighty or anywhere in between.

It's going to be a looong fucking night.

Chapter Seventeen

Mallory's first impression of the renowned rigger was that of a creepy middle-aged guy desperately trying to recapture his youth.

But she knew she'd have to keep it together so she didn't disappoint Kel. She wanted him to be proud of her, to do a good job so that, maybe, it'd give her a chance to be more to him than just a friend and roommate and play partner.

So after Jaymzon and his three guys brought their equipment into the club and got everything set up, and she'd filled out and signed all the release forms, she played along with Jaymzon's banter, his sexy teasing, his not-so-subtle innuendoes that probably worked on many of the models he dealt with.

She could play the game as well as anyone else.

But she kept her focus, whenever possible, firmly on Kel.

That was the only way she knew she wouldn't lose her composure and end up embarrassing herself and Kel, both.

Jaymzon wanted to start with the most difficult rigs first, progressing to the easier stuff later as energy levels and stamina lagged. During the first rig, which involved a crazy mix of colored plastic cling wrap, bubble wrap, chains, and some barbed wire, she forced her brain to settle and focus on memories of playing with Kel, how it felt to have his hands on her, ignoring the not-so-accidental incidental contact Jaymzon had with her breasts or between her legs while doing the initial rigging.

Kel acted very quiet. Whether because it was a shoot and he was trying to stay out of the way, or for some other reason, she couldn't tell. Although it seemed his usually placid expression looked far darker than she ever remembered.

Except for when he'd shown up to rescue her from her uncle.

Jaymzon was going for a weird industrial fusion vibe and had set up a chain fall to do the actual hoisting. She was a little surprised when Kel stepped in, insisting on fully testing the rig to his satisfaction before allowing the actual suspension to go forward.

Jaymzon stood there, arms crossed over his enormous and likely steroid-assisted pecs, as Kel checked it out.

"You don't think I know my job?" the older rigger asked.

Mallory suspected from the man's tone of voice that he wasn't used to people challenging him. And that he damn sure didn't like it.

Kel, outweighed and a couple of inches shorter than the man, didn't flinch. "She's *my* model," he said in a tone she didn't quite recognize. "You of all people should understand that responsibility. She's here because I asked her to fill in, and it's her first gig."

Well, okay, Kel hadn't exactly asked her, but Mallory wasn't about to correct him.

Jaymzon held up his palms, placating Kel. "Whoa, chill. Didn't mean any disrespect." Then the rigger looked at her, his gaze narrowing and a smile filling his face, chilling her.

Mallory fought the urge to shudder in revulsion.

* * * *

Fuck. Oh, fuck, oh fuck, oh fucking christ why the hell *did I tell him it was her first fucking gig?*

He might as well have dropped a slab of raw cow inside a pit of starving lions and expected them not to pounce. It'd been hard enough on him watching the man pawing at Mal while he'd rigged her. This was a far different scenario than when she played with his friends during a scene.

His friends weren't trying to poach her out from under him, were only interested in topping her, not taking her from him. His friends recognized boundaries and never did anything she didn't want done.

Jaymzon turned his back on Kel and walked over to where Mal was motionlessly waiting in the tied rig for the suspension portion to continue.

"Your very first gig, huh?" He chuckled. "Kel didn't warn me I had a virgin. Had I known that, I would have brought more gear. I'm always on the lookout for new talent."

Kel knew his next words risked farking both his relationship with Mal, as well as jeopardizing the job he was currently doing. "My other model flaked out at the last minute today. I couldn't get another one to replace her in time. When I said Mal is *my* model, I wasn't specific enough. Allow me to clarify. I meant Mal is *mine*."

Relief filled him as Jaymzon stopped in his tracks and turned to look at him. "She's *yours* yours?"

"That's right. She's *mine* mine. She belongs to *me*." At least the asshole recognized and respected protocols.

Usually.

The rigger's chin lifted as he stared down at Kel. "Is this going to be a problem?"

"If I thought it was going to be a problem, I wouldn't have agreed to let her do this shoot. As long as that boundary isn't going to be a problem for *you*. I apologize for not clarifying my relationship with her earlier, but I'm a professional, and I really didn't think it mattered in this case. Because it doesn't. I don't have a problem with her doing this gig or I never would have asked her to do it. She had the option to say no. I didn't force her to do this." In fact, Mallory had asked him to do it, but he wasn't about to tell the rigger that.

Jaymzon's guys silently watched them banter, their heads pivoting as if they were observing a tennis match. Kel didn't risk glancing at Mal to see how she'd reacted to his declaration.

All he cared about was not backing down from this guy. He didn't want to appear weak, but he also didn't want to appear to be some jealous fuck of a boyfriend, either. Riggers and photographers hated when boyfriends attended shoots with models. It rarely failed to fuck things up, especially if the boyfriends weren't in the lifestyle and didn't understand the intimate contact sometimes needed even when just tying a rig and not doing a sexual scene.

And the last thing Kel needed to get was a bad rep among professional riggers, and in the process fark any hopes of booking future fetish shoots with other big-name riggers.

* * * *

Mallory didn't dare breathe, didn't dare speak.

That one word, in Kel's voice, kept echoing through her brain. Her soul.

Mine.

She didn't know if he'd said it to stop the progressively creepy contact the rigger had been having with her, or if he'd really meant it.

Frankly, she didn't care at that moment.

Kel was looking out for her, protecting her. She'd take whatever she could get from him and clarify it later.

All that mattered was that they made it through the shoot without the rigger canceling or making her feel like she'd been groped by a senior citizen octopus.

The rigger finally answered. "It's not a problem for *me*. Like I said, I didn't even realize you two were an item."

She suspected now that the rigger had given ground, Kel would meet him halfway to smooth things over.

He didn't disappoint. "Like I said, my apologies for the confusion. I really wanted to do this shoot with you. It's not a problem for me, but her safety and welfare are my responsibility, as you can understand. I didn't mean for it to come off sounding like I didn't trust your skills." Kel shrugged, offering up a smile Mallory saw right through but suspected the other men wouldn't. "You know how it is. Never want to drop someone. I know how safety-conscious you are. It's one of the things I highly respect about you. But so am I, and I take my responsibility to her seriously. She has placed her trust in me. I won't violate that."

When Jaymzon nodded, she realized the rigger would be okay with this. Kel had offered up just enough ass-kissing to soothe the man's ego, while marking his territory in an unmistakable way.

"No hard feelings," Jaymzon said. Then he turned back to Mallory and smiled. "And my apologies if I overstepped any bounds."

Now she risked a glance at Kel, who imperceptibly tipped his chin in a nod. "It's okay," she said. "I was just really excited when he said I could do this. Your work is absolutely amazing…"

Sure enough, the groping stopped. And with her playing along like a star-struck teenybopper who'd scored backstage passes to a boy band concert, the rigger's mood quickly brightened even as he toned down the banter.

The rigging was difficult, uncomfortable, and in a few cases painful, despite the safety precautions and pre-rigging done before the actual suspensions.

By the time they finished in the wee hours before dawn, she realized she'd survived it and performed like a champ.

Kel led her over to one of the couches to curl up under a blanket while the men broke down their equipment and loaded up. Before leaving, Jaymzon walked over and deferred to Kel before squatting next to the couch and extending his hand to Mal.

"Beautiful shoot, Mallory," he said. "I wouldn't have known you'd never done a shoot before. You handled it like a pro. If you ever want to work with me again, it'd be my pleasure."

She shook with him. "Thank you. I have a fantastic teacher and rigger who showed me the ropes," she said, her gaze fixed firmly on Kel's face.

He smiled. A genuine, bright smile.

Jaymzon stood and offered his hand to Kel, who also shook with him. "You certainly have done a marvelous job working together," Jaymzon said. "And yes, I'd love to work with you again, too. It's refreshing to see there's someone who can mix work and their relationship and not let it fuck up either."

"Thanks."

Kel saw them out first. When he returned, he sat down on the end of the couch with Mallory's head in his lap. He laced his fingers through hers and brought them up to his mouth, feathering his lips across them.

"Guess we need to talk, huh?" he finally said, breaking the silence.

She swallowed. "Okay."

He gently squeezed her hands and seemed to be composing his thoughts. She didn't interrupt him.

"I made a rule after my last breakup not to get involved with anyone who didn't have their act together."

She felt her heart on the verge of breaking. "I understand," she whispered.

"Stop. Let me finish." He took a deep breath before looking into her eyes. "You're in a vulnerable place right now, emotionally, and with your life. I also don't want to be an idiot. Let's amend our original agreement, if you want to. Let's date. Take our time. There's no rush. I want our first time together to be perfect, but there's things you need to know about me before you decide if you want a relationship with me."

She'd swung from heartbreak to highest hopes in the space of a breath. "Okay."

"I don't have casual sex. I want to be in a relationship. But if you're going to be in a relationship with me, you need to know more about me. About the side of me you haven't seen yet."

"I want to see that side."

"You sure? It's dark and full of shadows."

She nodded.

He helped her sit up, then stood and offered her his hands. "Then let's go home and talk some more."

Chapter Eighteen

Despite her exhaustion, Mallory's brain raced, wired on adrenaline from his admission. Kel settled her on the couch before he went back downstairs to retrieve his laptop from the office.

When he sat next to her, he tucked her against his side, one arm draped around her shoulders. "It's okay if you change your mind," he said. "You won't hurt my feelings."

He typed in his password and navigated to a folder of pictures that needed yet another password to access.

In them, pictures not just of shibari, but of piercings, needle play, branding, cell popping.

Cutting.

He rested his head against hers. "This is me," he quietly said. "This is the darker side of me. It's easy to find people who want to model for something, or participate in a scene, but it's far more difficult to find someone who will tolerate a long-term partner who wants to turn them into their personal canvas on a regular basis."

She reached out and swiped through the pictures, entranced and terrified at the same time.

Terrified in the good way.

"We can still be friends and date and play partners and maybe even more, even if you don't want to do this," he said. "But I won't ever lie to you. I have to be honest with you that the person who becomes my life-partner needs to be able to deal with this part of me. Participate in it. Be okay with it."

She looked into his eyes again. "I trust you. I want to be with you."

"You *really* want to be with me?"

Mallory nodded, throat dry, heart racing.

He gently grasped her chin. "I thought you weren't into pain or edge play."

"I'm not. I mean, I don't get off on it like some people do."

"I don't want an unwilling partner."

"I *am* willing. I just need you to go slow, you know?"

"Have you ever tried needle play before?"

She shook her head.

"You might hate it."

"Won't know until I try."

"Why don't we start with something easier than that."

"Like what?"

"Knife play."

A shiver ran through her, from the tips of her toes to the roots of her hair. "Okay."

He smiled. "You ever do knife play before?"

"No. But I want to try it."

"Have you seen it before?"

"Yeah. Sensation and wet."

"Ah. You knew where I was going with that."

"I wouldn't mind a little blood and cutting, but nothing deep or detailed for my first one, please."

"Wise negotiation."

Who was she kidding? Just looking at him made her horny, the thought of him wanting her, wanting to play with her at least. She'd do nearly anything he asked of her.

Here, smuggle these Junior Mints into the movies for me in your purse.

Okay.

Here, rob this liquor store for me.

Okay.

Well, okay, not the second one. Not that he'd ever ask her to do that.

But she'd definitely smuggle chocolate into a theatre for him.

Hell, she'd smuggle a gallon of milk and a bottle of chocolate sauce into a theatre for him just so he could have chocolate milk, if he wanted it.

I'm sick.

"Are you even attracted to me?" she asked. "Or are you just attracted to the fact that I'm someone different to play with?"

His expression softened. Before she realized what he was doing, he'd leaned in and placed a slow, gentle, tender kiss on her lips.

"I'm attracted to *you*. Every bit of you. And if you can't see that, I don't know what I can do to prove it to you. If we're going to have any hope of being together, you have to be able to trust me. Part of that is being able to take me at my word. Can you do that?"

She nodded.

* * * *

Kel wondered how she'd feel during the actual act. If she'd still feel the same.

"Tonight—rather, this morning—we both need sleep. You need a long, warm shower first, or you're going to feel like a block of the bad kind of pain when you get up."

He shut down the laptop and set it on the coffee table. Then he took her into his arms. "So, for now, we'll go slow. I don't want to do anything until we've eased into this next stage. You'll need at least a few days to recover from tonight. But for the time being, I'm yours, and you're mine. Boyfriend and girlfriend."

"Submissive?"

He hesitated. "Let's hold off on that. That's a serious commitment to me. I don't go around slapping collars on people. Let's see if you even like the real me first."

He waited to go to bed until he heard her finish with her shower and retire to her own bedroom.

Then he took a hot shower, rubbing one out in the process while thinking about how gorgeous she had looked wrapped in barbed wire, and then collapsed onto his bed to try to sleep.

When he awoke a little after noon, there were still no signs of life from her room. He quietly got up, dressed, and fixed himself a bowl of cereal to take down to the office.

Down there, he started working processing the shots from the night before, his cock thickening in his shorts as he studied her body.

She.

Was.

Fucking.

Gorgeous.

She brought a natural vulnerability to the shots that only amplified the rigging Jaymzon had used on her.

These images were going to be hot and widely received.

On the flip side of that, he knew the inevitable, that people would grab and post them on their own FetLife profiles, make obscene comments about her and the poses, and distribute them all over the place even though it was illegal to copy and post them, a violation of copyright.

Everyone, able to stare at her, to see her in a way usually only he did.

This was different. She was *his*. He could twist it into any semantics he wanted, but she *was* his. He wanted her. Maybe even needed her just a little.

Maybe she'd been his all along and he'd been too stubborn to admit it to himself.

As long as she could tolerate his dark side, learn to love playing in the shadows with him, enjoy her time there with him.

If she could...

He sat back and stared at one shot of her, a close-up he'd taken for himself of her face, her eyes half-closed, lips parted, a little fear and discomfort there, the salt in the cookie dough recipe, making it that much sweeter.

Richer.

Beautiful.

After he finished processing the shots, he put duplicates of them on a thumb drive for her to have, if she wanted them. He'd just made it upstairs a little before three when he heard her bedroom door open.

He walked down to greet her. She wore the blue satin robe.

Dammit, I love that thing.

"How are you feeling?"

"Sore." She offered him a smile when he opened his arms to her. She slipped into his embrace, her face pressed against his chest, her arms wrapped around him.

"How'd you sleep?"

"Good. Maybe the best I've slept in a while." She finally tipped her face up to his and he kissed her, unsuccessfully trying to will his cock to stand down.

"Oh." He fished the thumb drive out of his pocket and handed it to her. "Pictures. Your copies from last night. You can leave the thumb drive on my desk when you're finished."

"Thank you."

He kissed her one last time, then patted her on the ass. "Go do whatever you were going to do before I interrupted you. I'll fix you some breakfast."

He loved her smile. It just might be his undoing. "Thank you, Sir."

Hell, he loved hearing her call him Sir, even if she wasn't formally his submissive.

He waited until she closed the bathroom door to return to the kitchen, whistling as he went.

If this was the next stage of his life, maybe he'd just found a level above Heaven that he'd never dreamed existed before.

Chapter Nineteen

Kel lasted another two weeks at the boyfriend-girlfriend level before he couldn't take it anymore. He'd shown her all his private edge play pictures and she hadn't been scared away yet. He showed her his supplies, explained various things to her, and still she insisted she wanted to try it. They'd gone through sexual history discussions with each other, and even though both of them had previous clean tests, he paid for them to both get tested again, a full STD panel, the results of which they'd have back the next week.

She'd had three partners before him, but one had been in high school, and the other two over a year before.

He wouldn't deny he'd enjoy showing her things she'd never experienced before.

On the other side of that, he sincerely hoped she still wanted him when all was said and done.

Friday morning, Kel pulled her to him after breakfast. "Any plans for tonight?"

Mallory shook her head. "No. I work until six and then I'm all yours."

He leaned in and kissed her. "Then I think tonight we need to start exploring a little more. When you get home, take a shower, no makeup, and come downstairs wearing your blue robe."

She nodded, her cheeks flushing.

Her smile lighting his soul.

That evening, Kel cleared out space downstairs in his workshop and set out the MMA mats he sometimes used for rigging before laying down black fabric over them. As he prepared the other items and got the lights and cameras positioned, he felt nervous, giddy, and just a wee bit nauseous.

Maybe this is true love.

When Mal emerged from the stairwell, he understood the cliché about a person's heart hitting their feet. In this case, in a good way.

She wasn't just beautiful, she looked stunning, her blue satin robe shimmering in the light. He'd put on Steely Dan to play by, one of his favorite bands, not needing to impress anyone and wanting the mood perfectly set. It also helped mask the sounds of the music pulsing through the wall from the club on the other side.

The final thing he needed, he threw down several large pillows onto the mats.

She stood there, waiting for his direction. He walked over and took her hands. "You sure about this?"

She met his gaze without hesitation. "I trust you. I want to do this."

He stroked her cheek. As he'd asked, she wasn't wearing any makeup. He reached up and gently removed the elastic band from her hair, combing it out with his fingers so it cascaded down her shoulders. "Did I ever tell you how much I love this color on you?"

She rewarded him with a smile. "Thank you, Sir."

He leaned in and kissed her, slowly, gently, savoring it. He wanted to cherish every second of this with her. "If you change your mind at any point, just say red, and I'll stop. About anything. Promise me. Just like any other time we play. You won't disappoint me if you call it."

"I promise." She unfastened the belt of her robe and shrugged it off, letting it fall to the floor behind her. "I want this, and I want you. I want all of you, the real you. I want to be the person you can let go with, just like I want you to be the person I can let go to. I want to play in the shadows with you."

He cupped her cheek in his hand and kissed her, a little harder, nipping her lower lip and sucking on it before lifting his head again and staring into her eyes. "I'm going to put my marks on you," he whispered. "I'm going to paint my feelings onto your flesh." He reached down and rested his hands on her hips, trailing his fingers lightly over and up her rounded tummy, to her breasts, and down her sides until they settled on her ass.

He dug his fingers in, mindful not to mark her yet, wanting the before and after clearly delineated in the photos. "I mark what's mine," he said. "And if we're going to do this, that means we're going to be monogamous to each other. And more, it means we both get veto power over anyone the other plays with. You don't want to do that, you don't screw around behind my back. You talk to me and we deal with it. I won't screw around behind your back, either. We're adults. You want to be in a relationship with me, it means we communicate our needs. I ever catch you breaking that trust, that's it. Not saying you have to pledge undying love to me, but I will give you one hundred percent of my trust and respect, and I promise in return to respect you and not to break your trust. Deal?"

She nodded, her beautiful smile melting his soul. "I don't want anyone but you." She reached down and grabbed the bulge pressing against the front of his jeans, squeezing just a little. "I'm more than happy to take what I can get and be happy for it."

He barely managed to hold back his needy moan. It would be too easy to throw her down on the mats and fuck her silly right then.

Who was he kidding? He knew he loved her. He just couldn't bring himself to say it out loud yet. The last time he'd thought he was in love, he'd ended up with a woman who was five gallons of crazy in a two-gallon bucket.

But he'd meant every word he said. He wouldn't screw around on her, and maybe she'd put up with him long enough for him to finally feel secure saying those three little words to her.

Meanwhile, if nothing else, he'd *show* her how he felt. He led her over to the pillows and arranged her how he wanted on her back, getting the cameras ready and focused. He'd use a remote to trigger them, and then a hand-held camera for the close-ups he wanted.

Already, the thought of going through post to edit the photos had him hard and throbbing.

He started by using royal blue rope on her lower arms, tying gauntlets around her wrists and then raising her arms over her head and tying them together.

Her focus never left him. Every time he looked, her blue gaze lay upon him like a sensual cloud.

Then he tied gauntlets around her feet and ankles, bringing up first her right foot, then her left, bending her legs at the knees and tying her feet to her thighs as closely as he knew her muscles could stand.

More pictures.

He pushed her legs apart, propped up by pillows so she could hold the pose longer.

His heart pounded in his chest at how open, vulnerable she looked.

Beautiful. A perfect goddess with flaming red hair, ready for him to take her.

Wanting him to take her.

He took several close-up shots of how the rope pressed into the flesh of her upper thighs before setting the camera aside and kneeling between her legs.

"Color."

"Green," she whispered.

He slid his fingers up her body, to her breasts, grabbing and squeezing, his gaze never leaving hers, watching, gauging.

Only when she bit down on her lower lip did he stop applying pressure, holding it there, watching as her flesh started changing color under his fingers from creamy white to pink. Her nipples stood out, hard and peaked, inviting.

He leaned in and flicked his tongue over first one, then the other, before releasing her and sitting up again. The soft gasps she made sent throbbing agony through his cock and balls. He wanted to fuck her. He wanted to fuck her hard and fast and make her his, with his fingers digging into her flesh and leaving his fingerprints all over her even as he made her come.

He grabbed the camera and took pictures of her breasts before the imprints of his fingers there faded.

Putting it aside again, he scooted back just enough he could lean in and kiss her pussy.

The louder moan he drew from her nearly made him come in his jeans.

Swiping his tongue up her clit, he lifted his head to watch as her body flushed, deep red creeping into her pussy lips, her clit swelling.

He buried his face between her thighs, keeping his eyes open so he could look up her body and watch her expression.

Something between shock and ecstasy swept across her features before she closed her eyes and let out a long, low cry as her orgasm hit.

That's what I wanted to hear.

When he was sure she'd finished cresting that wave, he turned his head to the side and bit down, hard, on the tender flesh of the inside of her left thigh, her moan turning into a cry. He turned his head to the other side and repeated it, barely remembering to grab the camera and take pictures.

Putting it aside again, he worked his way up her flesh from her mound to her breasts, biting, pinching, squeezing, marking her, drawing cries from her that turned to moans every time he'd reach down between her legs and slide two fingers into her pussy, finger-fucking her just to the point of coming again before stopping. Denying.

Holding her back until he was ready to let her come again.

He wanted her next orgasm to be with his cock deeply embedded inside her.

Her expression had taken on a deliciously crazed combination between agony and delight, her lower lip lightly swollen from where she kept biting down on it.

He leaned in and kissed her, sucking on it, nibbling, licking.

Then he worked his way up the insides of her arms, each set of marks he left in her flesh silently branding her as his, his mouth going back and forth between sucking on her nipples to biting her arms just to the point before breaking skin.

Every time his hand traveled back between her legs, her hips flexed, rocking, her entire body consumed with the motion, trying to get herself off before the inevitable stoppage and denial.

He finally pulled his hand from her pussy, slipping his fingers between her lips so she could suck her juices off them. As he did, he took more close-ups, getting the detail of how her lips folded around his flesh.

With the camera once again set aside, he reached for his knife, the small, sharp stiletto he'd never used on anyone else for knife play.

Yet.

* * * *

Mal gasped at the sensation of the cool, flat steel of the blade pressing against her stomach when he laid it there.

"Don't move," he whispered, a smile crossing his face. "It's very, very sharp."

She swallowed hard. The first orgasm had hit her like a runaway train, the best damn one of her life.

Then he'd started the tease and denial and her pussy ached to be filled, her clit throbbing harder every time he built her up just to stop.

He took another round of pictures before adjusting the pillows behind her head.

"Don't close your eyes," he said. "I want you to watch me. I want you to see what I do. I want to know you're okay with everything I'm doing."

She nodded, unable to not see the sharp blade lying on her stomach.

He picked it up and then dipped his head, burying his tongue in her pussy again. The man had a mouth even more talented than his fingers and hands, and he quickly built her up—

Before sitting up again, leaving her almost near tears as he once again denied her.

"Color."

"Green!" she gasped.

He changed position, stretching out on his left side, his arm hooked under and around her right leg. The weight of his body pressed against her knee, spreading her even wider than before.

"Keep your legs open," he warned. "And do not move. This blade is very, very sharp."

Then he brought up the knife with his right hand.

Slowly, he touched the tip of it to her flesh, lightly at first and then applying just a little more pressure until it bit through the surface, a tiny line of blood welling up.

"Make all the noise you want," he said, his voice thick and yet teasing. "I want to hear you."

The cries escaped her as pain built, tears rolling down her face, not even as bad as a heavy caning but not being able to move had added an extra degree of edge for her. And she damn sure wouldn't safeword for it, either. It wasn't a large shape, and it wasn't a deep cut. When he finished a few minutes later the small heart lay clearly outlined on her flesh, defined by her blood.

He set the knife aside and snapped several pictures, keeping his left arm hooked around her leg. Only when he was satisfied did he put the camera aside and stand up, slowly unbuttoning his shirt.

"*My* marks, all over you," he softly said. "Mine. For as long as you want to be mine." He dropped the shirt off to the side and started working on his jeans. "Mine to mark, mine to design," he softly said, kicking his jeans and briefs off to join his shirt. He reached over and grabbed a condom pouch, ripping it open and rolling it slowly down his shaft.

He knelt between her legs again and swiped the head of his cock up and down along her pussy lips, her juices freely flowing and coating his cock.

He traced his finger along the heart, where the bleeding was already beginning to stop, and covered his finger with her blood. He drew a small K on her chest, between her breasts, smiling as he did. Only then did he thrust his hips forward, slowly impaling her with his cock, filling her, making her cry out again, in pleasure this time.

He filled her, stretching her in a delicious way she'd never felt before. Not even the vibrator hidden in her dresser drawer was quite this big or felt this good.

Bracing himself with his hands planted on either side of her head, he looked down at her. "Now you can come again," he whispered before leaning in and kissing her.

As he did, he slowly withdrew his cock before plunging in again, over and over, the angle and her swollen, exposed clit conspiring together to quickly drive her toward release. His tongue fucked her mouth, hard, fast, brutally, even as his cock fucked her slowly, tenderly, patiently, until she hit the point of no return. Not as hard an orgasm as the one he'd driven her to with his mouth, but even sweeter.

He lifted his mouth from hers. "That's it. Your body knows who owns you, doesn't it? Who you belong to. Who knows how to give you what you need." He started fucking her hard, fast, deep, brutally, driving her across the mats with each thrust until he hooked his arms under her shoulders and held her in place.

And still, she kept coming, never before realizing how good it could feel like this, how fantastic sex with the right partner could be. Her tears still fell, this time of pleasure as she cried out. Kel's fingers dug into the top of her shoulders, clawing as he let out a loud cry of his own and his body fell rigid and still on top of hers. Breathing heavily, he rested his forehead against hers, noses touching.

"Mine," he whispered. "My beautiful, gorgeous canvas."

"Yours," she whispered back. "Only yours."

Chapter Twenty

After disposing of the condom, he untied her legs, taking several rounds of pictures of the ligature marks before rubbing her flesh to help get the color and circulation back.

Her arms he kept bound.

She soon found out why.

He rolled her onto her knees, ass in the air, legs spread. She heard him take more pictures before his fingers returned to her pussy, playing with her clit, finger-fucking her again, quickly bringing her to the brink.

But this time he didn't stop. He sank his teeth into the flesh of her ass, making her cry out both in pleasure and in pain as her pussy clamped down on his fingers.

"That's it," he murmured. "I want the thought of me touching you, no matter in what way, to get you wet." He bit her again, and again, relentlessly making her come as he did. Even to the point she heard a vibrator click on and he slid it inside her pussy and held it there as he bit his way up her spine toward her shoulders.

A pause for her to catch her breath as he took more close-ups. He pulled the vibrator away and she heard the sound of another condom pouch being opened before his cock easily slid into her exposed cunt.

"Hold still, baby," he whispered. She suspected what was coming next when he brushed her hair away from her back.

And then the feel of cold steel pressed against her right shoulder.

"As above, so below," he softly said before she felt the tip of the knife bite into her again.

He whispered soft, loving encouragement as he carved another shape into the back of her right shoulder, his cock never softening inside her. She didn't move, barely dared to breathe. Whether it was the effects of deep subspace, or she was growing more used to the pain, this one didn't hurt even a fraction as much as the one on her thigh.

Once he set the blade aside he took more pictures. Then she heard the vibrator click on again.

"You are a masterpiece," he whispered, reaching under her with the vibrator and pressing it against her clit as he slowly fucked her. "*My* masterpiece."

She gave up, gave over all control to him. It wasn't any use trying to think she'd never be able to come again, because he wanted it, and he would have it.

Her body responded, his cock slowly fucking her as she orgasmed over and over. Only when he was ready did he turn the vibrator off, dig his fingers deep into the flesh of her hips, and fuck her once more.

Owned. Desired. Beautiful. His body couldn't lie any more than hers could. When he came inside her, he held himself buried deep in her pussy, folding his body around hers, one last bite delivered to the back of her left shoulder.

He rolled her with him onto the mats, onto her left side, cradled against him as he reached up and untied her arms. Then he pulled out, one more biting kiss against the side of her neck as he went to clean up and grab the camera.

She let him move her, position her, document his new ownership of her and her body, his visible claims to her.

She had no desire to have anyone's hands on her besides his. Right now, she recognized the mental flight, the flood of endorphins surging through her, subspace deeper than any she'd ever known before. Even the cuttings on her shoulder and thigh didn't feel any worse than a dull ache, no more pain than the bite marks now covering her flesh.

After turning off the lights and cameras, he caught her hands and pulled her to her feet, her arms draped around his neck as he grabbed her ass and held her tightly pressed to him. In the background, the music finally returned to focus in her brain as they slowly swayed in time to it.

When he kissed her, tenderly, exploring her once more, she melted. Without a word he folded her against his side, his arm around her waist, and led her upstairs to his bathroom.

After putting her in the shower, he went to the cabinet and retrieved gauze and alcohol before joining her in the shower. "This is going to sting," he said, smiling.

"Like that breaks your heart."

"Not at all." He knelt in front of her. She spread her legs so he could reach her inner thigh, and yes, it stung like a motherfucker, but he blew on it even as he swabbed it clean. He repeated it with her shoulder, and it was only when he finished that she realized she was, impossibly, horny again.

He'd noticed. Hard not to notice it when her juices slowly dripped from her with her legs spread.

"Lean forward," he ordered. "Hands against the wall."

She did. He stepped out of the shower and returned with another condom.

"You have stock in those, I hope?" She'd gotten a prescription for birth control pills from the doctor they'd gone to, but they wouldn't be safe to have unprotected sex for several weeks yet.

He smiled. "I think we need to get fluid bonded sooner rather than later or we're going to go broke. Come on, test results." He rolled the condom on, nudging her feet a little farther apart before sliding his cock into her pussy.

They both moaned as he filled her. He stroked his fingers up her back, avoiding the mark he'd cut into her, then raked his nails down her flesh again.

"You can't lie to me," he said. "I felt the way your pussy contracted around me." He did it again, and again, even as he slowly fucked her. "I mean it. I want to get you to the point that every time I touch you, pleasure or pain, your body wants it, aches for it." He reached around her, finding her clit and rolling it between his fingers. "Give me one more right now. You know you want to."

She did. Or, her body, at least, wanted it. When she cried out, he waited for her to finish before grabbing her hips and fucking her hard and fast, filling the condom as his balls emptied inside her.

He pulled her up against his body, his hands cupping her breasts. "I have to be honest with you about something," he said.

"What?" A little tendril of fear filled her. This sounded like a confession.

"Normally I'm not good for more than one or two a night," he said, nipping her shoulder. "Don't be disappointed if I can't perform like this every night. It's been a while for me, and you're just too damn beautiful."

* * * *

Kel pulled out as she turned in his arms, a gorgeous smile on her face. "Yeah, well, I suspect tomorrow I'm going to be sore and not very bendy."

"I'll help you work out the kinks."

"I'm sure you will."

He cleaned up and started the shower, holding her under the warm water, taking his time washing her body, her hair, exploring, loving her.

He did love her. He'd be stupid to deny it to himself even if he couldn't admit it to her yet.

After drying her and him off and putting antibiotic ointment and large bandages on her cuttings, he led her into his bedroom, tucking her into bed before cradling her against him, spooning with her.

He tenderly kissed the back of her neck. "Sleep well, my beautiful goddess."

She snuggled even more tightly against him. "You, too, Sir."

His eyes popped open. They still hadn't discussed titles between them. Even though she wasn't officially collared to him, he realized he'd easily slipped into an ownership role with her.

And it was one he hoped he never had to relinquish.

One more kiss, to the top of her head. "For as long as you'll have me," he whispered.

* * * *

The next morning, he awoke before she did and slipped out of bed without disturbing her. He ran downstairs for his camera and returned upstairs, pleased to find her still asleep. The light was exactly right, golden in the viewfinder as he took pictures of her sleeping form, easing the sheet down her body without waking her.

Perfection.

He knelt next to the bed, his chin on the mattress and staring at her sleeping face when she opened her eyes. She let out a soft laugh. "You just took pictures of me, didn't you?"

"Uh, to quote your bestie, duh."

When worry clouded her features, he leaned in and kissed her. "You're beautiful. You are a goddess, in my eyes. You're *my* goddess if I say you are."

"Sir's always right?" It was more a question than a statement.

"I think I like that rule."

She giggled. "Shit," she muttered. "I walked into *that* one."

"Yes, you did." He brought the camera up before she could open her eyes and got a picture of her delicious, sleepy smile. "How do you feel?" He set the camera on the dresser and stood, pulling the sheet the rest of the way off her.

She stretched, wincing. Soft, hazy bruises marked her arms and legs where he'd had her tied. Bite marks were visible all up and down her body everywhere he looked.

The faint impression of his fingers ringed her breasts and marked her hips. When he looked at her back, he could also see where he'd raked his nails down her flesh.

She sat up. "Want me to take care of that for you?" She wore a playful smile as she pointed at his erection.

"Actually, yeah. Stay right there." He retrieved a condom from the bathroom and then held out a hand to help her from the bed and onto her knees.

He handed the pouch to her. "Sorry it's not flavored."

"I could just do this the old-fashioned way, you know."

He smiled. "A—I'm a sadist. B—not until we're fluid-bonded."

"I trust you."

"I know you do. That's why we're going to wait the little bit of time it takes to get all our test results back."

"But you went down on me."

"That was my risk to assume," he said. "Are you arguing with me?"

"No, Sir."

He grabbed two fistfuls of her hair. "Good girl. Just wait, when we do get to that point, you're going to get tied up tightly and well-fucked and filled with my cum in every hole, until I can't get it up anymore. Mouth first, then your pussy, and then that sweet, gorgeous ass of yours. And only then will I untie you. And while I'm waiting to get it back up between fuckings, I'll work you over with a vibrator and make sure you get that gorgeous subby glaze in your eyes."

A beautiful flush filled her cheeks now. It went nicely with the nice subby glaze she was already getting in her eyes right that moment. "Yes, Sir."

"Good girl. Now roll that condom on me and suck my cock."

He loved how her fingers trembled as she did it. He added an extra skills test by nudging her knees wider apart with his foot and then running his big toe up and down her clit, along her pussy lips.

Oh, she was already wet. Deliciously soaked, her juices practically dripping from her.

When she had the condom rolled down his shaft and wrapped her lips around the tip, he held her there with his hands in her hair. "I'm driving," he said, knowing this wouldn't take long.

She was just too damn beautiful for him to hold back.

He started slow and easy, fucking just the head of his cock between her lips, going deeper and deeper with each stroke, not wanting to gag her and yet wanting to fill her mouth and throat with every inch of his meat. Just the thought of how gorgeous she would look swallowing his cum set off his orgasm even faster than he'd planned. He pushed in deeper as his cock throbbed inside the condom, his balls emptying and filling it, holding her still until he was finished.

When he pulled out, he leaned in and kissed her. "Sorry. Didn't realize I'd come quite that fast."

"I take it as a compliment."

"You should." He sucked on her lower lip. "Up on the bed on your back. Legs apart. I'll be right back."

He was getting his exercise that morning. He cleaned up and ran downstairs, naked, to fetch some ropes.

He found her waiting, exactly the way he'd left her, on her back on the bed. He quickly tied her hands over her head, and tied her legs similarly to the way he'd tied them the night before, only looser, allowing her a little more movement.

He settled in. "My turn." Yes, he'd taken a calculated risk by going down on her, but he suspected she wouldn't have lied about her past six months of sexual activity and that the tests would come back next week clean.

Until then, he would enjoy himself. He sucked and nibbled on her sensitive clit, making her come several times, until she started trying to twist away from him.

He pinched the inside of her left thigh, hard. "Stop moving. Unless you're safewording, I get as many orgasms out of you as I want." He held her legs down with his arms, pinning her with the weight of his body as he coaxed her into one last orgasm that left her sobbing under him on the bed.

He untied her and cuddled her close as she rolled to bury her face against his chest.

"Good?" He stroked her back, relishing the teeth marks he knew were there even though he couldn't see them at that moment.

"Yes, Sir," she whispered. "The best ever."

* * * *

That was no lie. He was the. Best. Ever.

Ever.

That'd she'd had, at least. No, she wasn't exactly a slut, or even very experienced, but she damn sure knew a good orgasm when she felt one.

She'd been relying on giving them to herself for so damn long, she should know when one felt good or not.

And he felt good.

Everything about him was good.

Even the dark and shadowy parts.

She wanted to spend more time playing with him in the dark spaces, let him do what he wanted to her body.

Because for the first time that she could remember, she felt alive in a way she'd never dreamed before. Just when she thought things in her life were going well, they got even better.

She only hoped he didn't get tired of her.

Chapter Twenty-One

They finally made it into the shower and out to breakfast. Mallory wore a long gypsy skirt and a loose mid-sleeve tunic that helped hide nearly all her marks.

What she hadn't counted on was Kel taking her shopping.

"You need something to wear to the club tonight," he said.

"Sir?" It felt natural and right to call him that, even though they hadn't formally discussed titles.

She figured if he had a problem with it, he would have said something about it sooner. So until Kel objected, Sir he would be to her.

It comforted her.

"Little sundress," he said. "Something skimpy to show off your marks."

Heat filled her face as she glanced around the restaurant. No one had heard their discussion.

He smiled and leaned in. "I want everyone to see as much of you as they can." He arched his eyebrows at her. "Unless you want to be completely naked all night?"

She shook her head, hard, even though his playfully evil grin told her he wouldn't make her do that.

He captured her hand over the table and brushed his fingers along her knuckles. "I am going to strip you," he whispered. "I'm going to tie you, suspend you, and make you come over and over again." He brought her hand up to his lips and kissed it. "And everyone's going to see the marks I've already put on you and know exactly who owns you. And everyone there will know I belong to you, too. Every woman in the room is going to envy you and wish they were you. And most of the men will probably be jealous that I'm the one playing with you."

It didn't seem possible that her clit could stand up and holla after all the attention it'd received the night before and that morning.

Holla.

Oh, boy.

He grinned as he sat back, releasing her hand.

Oh, boy *oh boy.*

* * * *

Kel was a man of his word, too. Mallory thought for sure when he pulled her car into the parking lot of the adult store on US 41 that she'd be in the clear. It sold everything from sexy clothes to party favors and adult toys. She and Chelbie had gone there once looking for corsets. Chelbie's solid size-twelve body had easily fit into several.

There'd been very little, except shoes, that Mallory had been able to wear.

Apparently, they'd improved their selection in the two years since she'd last visited the location. They had a variety of club and dance wear, including a plus-sized section. That was exactly where Kel led her, releasing her hand only so he could start browsing the rack.

A saleswoman walked over to help. By that time, Kel already had five selections for Mallory to try on. Wearing a playfully predatory grin, he followed Mallory as she followed the saleswoman to one of the two dressing rooms and tried the first one on.

It was cut from black metallic fabric, damned slinky thing, with a keyhole top that tied at the back of her neck, barely anything covering her breasts, and which led to a skirt consisting of four panels. It showed every curve and roll and stretch mark and she felt fat in it.

When she stepped out to show him, he smiled. "Perfect. Next one."

"You *like* this?"

The saleswoman was talking to another couple browsing corsets. Kel stepped close, grabbed Mallory's hand, and pressed it against the front of his jeans so she could feel the outline of his stiff cock.

"That don't lie." He quickly released her hand and stepped back. His tone dropped into what she was quickly coming to think of as his Sir mode. "We're *getting* it. Now try. The next. One on."

She dove back into the dressing room, hands shaking as she tried to get out of the thing and finally having to shove it all down her legs so she could step out of it.

The next four selections received a thumbs-up from him as well. When she emerged from the dressing room in her street clothes, he took the five dresses from her and headed for the checkout counter. After they were safely ensconced in her car with the AC running, he grinned at her.

"You really have no idea how sexy I think you are, do you?"

"Not dressed in those," she muttered.

He gently turned her chin so she was forced to look at him. His playful grin had fled, replaced by dead-serious Dom face. "Are you saying my opinion isn't valid to you?"

"What? No, I'm not saying that at all."

"Good." He leaned in and kissed her. "Then when I say I think something makes you look sexy, that's all that matters. If you're going to give your body to me, I get to make the call when it comes to that. When it comes to going to fetish events, I get the final say on what you wear. Understand?" He leveled the force of his brown gaze at her.

She nodded. This was what she'd wanted. She trusted him. She had to let go of this and move on if she ever wanted to grow as a person, and she knew that.

The rest of her life needed to be lived for her and her happiness, not for anyone else.

His smile returned. "Good girl. I know what looks sexy. I'm the only one who should matter when it comes to that. Right?"

"Yes, Sir."

One last kiss, and he sat back to buckle his seat belt. "Good girl. You'll wear the blue one tonight. No panties. When I tie you, it's going to be with you fully naked."

She didn't know if her nerves would take it, but she wouldn't safeword for it.

"Yes, Sir."

* * * *

They swung by and picked up Chelbie on their way to Sigalo's. Her parents weren't home when they knocked on the front door and Chelbie let them in and hugged them. When Mallory winced as Chelbie's hand hit the bandage on the back of her right shoulder, Chelbie noticed.

Her eyes narrowed as she frowned. "What happened?"

"*I* happened," Kel said, lacing fingers with Mallory. He brought her hand to his lips and kissed it.

Chelbie's gaze narrowed even more as she looked from him to Mallory and back. The grin slowly spread over her face like a spill of honey across the floor, until it lit her eyes and she let out a delighted laugh. "Shut. *Up*. You did *not*?"

He squeezed Mallory's hand. "Mal, you want to lift your skirt and show her?"

Her face felt like a supernova had gone off, but she lifted the skirt's hem so Chelbie could see the line of bite marks along her inner right thigh, up to where the bandage covered her mark there. He'd checked and redressed them before they left. Neither showed any sign of infection, and both were already scabbed over and healing nicely.

"No. Way." Chelbie smacked his shoulder with the back of her hand. "Dude, you rock."

"May I drop my skirt now, Sir?" Mallory asked.

"Yes, you may."

Chelbie let out a squeal and threw her arms around Mallory again. "I'm so happy for you guys! Oh my god, please tell me I can be there so I can see Slimon's face when you tell him you're an item and he can go jump off a dock."

* * * *

Mallory's nerves fluttered as they entered the club that night. She headed to the bathroom to go change into the blue dress, *sans* panties, as he'd ordered.

She also peeled off the bandages on her shoulder and inner thigh.

Chelbie leaned in to examine them. "Wow. I didn't know he was into cutting. I mean, I'd heard about needles and piercing, but wow. Did it hurt?"

Mal craned her neck to look at the one on her shoulder in the mirror. "In all the good ways," she said with a smile.

Looking back on it, she honestly hadn't felt much more pain than she did when getting caned or paddled. It had been absorbed in the sweet flood of endorphins.

"You look sexeh, girlie," Chelbie said as she examined the dress. "He took you shopping, didn't he?"

She blushed as she shoved her street clothes into the tote bag she'd brought with her. "Yes."

"You don't sound happy."

"I don't feel sexy, even though I've been ordered to let him make the call."

"He's right. You do look sexy. If I was gay or bi, girlie, I'd do you."

"We need to get you laid."

"Side topic, although not entirely wrong, either. I'd suggest you get your tushy out there before he comes in here looking for you."

He'd already set up the A-frame and had his ropes ready. When he saw her emerge from the bathroom, he crooked his finger at her from across the room.

She went, her focus only on him, not on anyone else there. They could have had the club to themselves for all she cared.

He smiled as she walked up to him. When he grabbed her and kissed her, his fingers digging into her ass, she felt his cock harden in his jeans.

"That's what you do to me, baby," he whispered into her ear. "So don't ever tell me you're not sexy."

He quickly stripped the dress off her and started tying her. She kept her focus on him, not the increasingly large crowd gathering around them. Tony and Seth were spotting and keeping people back, as was Chelbie.

Although she suspected Chelbie would be a lot scarier to someone getting too close than Tony or Seth would.

Kel tied her, the chest harness also holding her breasts captive, sticking out and ready for him to torment.

Then, he suspended her. But unlike other times, he tied her legs, too, so they were spread and she couldn't pull them together. He also used paracord to tie her hair, holding her head up and back. Then he tied her arms against her sides, totally immobilizing her.

That was when she heard the *click*. He stepped in close, one hand reaching beneath her to fondle her breasts while the other slid the humming vibrator between her legs. He gently rocked her, until her body was fucking the vibrator and his hand held still.

"Come for me, my beautiful goddess," he whispered in her ear. "Let them see who owns you. Come for me."

She closed her eyes, her body giving in, giving up, giving him what he wanted. Everything he wanted. The first orgasm rolled through her as he whispered in her ear all the things he would do to her once they were back home and alone. She wasn't even aware at first how much he had her swinging back and forth now, the vibrator fucking her deeply with every stroke.

He nipped the shell of her ear, not letting up until he'd drawn a cry from her. "My marks on you, my ropes on you, my sweet, delicious living canvas."

His tone as much as his words drove her hard and deep into subspace.

Didn't hurt that the vibrator had her coming over and over again, one long, rolling release, a wave of pleasure that seemed to have no beginning, no end.

She didn't know how long she hung there, only that she never wanted it to end. When he finally pulled the vibrator away and turned it off, she wasn't even sure she had the strength to open her eyes, much less walk under her own power.

He quickly untied her hair, her arms, her legs, gently lowering her, easing her down onto a towel he had ready for her. He draped a blanket around her and then worked to untie her and put his ropes up. Only when he was ready did he help her up, with Tony and Seth grabbing his bags for him, and guide her over to one of the couches where she curled up with her head in his lap, her back turned to the rest of the room.

His fingers buried in her hair, gently tugging. "Such a gorgeous girl," he said. "So beautiful."

She closed her eyes, surfing subspace. "Thank you, Sir."

He leaned in and kissed her. "*My* girl."

She snuggled closer, a smile on her face. "*Your* girl."

* * * *

A mix of emotions filled Kel as he scened with her. Pride in her trust in him, pride in the way men and women both eyed her while they scened, and a tiny touch territorial.

Mine.

Okay, maybe more than a touch territorial.

Way more.

When he got her back home and in his bed, he used the vibrator on her again, knowing she was nearing the point of collapse for the night but wanting to hear her come one more time before he wrapped his cock in a condom and fucked her, hard and fast, with her ankles slung over his shoulders and while biting down on the side of her right breast, hard enough to make her cry out one last time as he exploded and filled the condom.

Only then did he gather her into his arms, his body spooned around hers.

"Sleep, goddess," he whispered.

Already, his mind was filled with the things he wanted to do to her on Sunday, all day. They both had to work next week, so his time with her would be a little more limited.

He wanted to make the most of this that he could, while he could.

All the while praying she never changed her mind about him, or about playing in the shadows with him.

Chapter Twenty-Two

Mallory awoke late Sunday morning sore in all the good ways. Kel wasn't in bed, and she didn't hear him upstairs, so she guessed he'd gone downstairs to the office. After using the bathroom and finding her robe, she wandered out to the kitchen.

He called up to her. "You awake?"

She smiled at his hopeful tone. "Yes, Sir."

"Good. I was about to come play with you if you didn't wake up soon." He joined her upstairs, kissing her good morning, fisting her hair as he did. "Good morning, gorgeous."

"Good morning, Sir."

"If there's anything you want to do before I start having my way with you again," he teased, "I suggest you do it."

"I need to go online and check my bank balance," she said. "And I want to look at my student account. I need to see if he's paid my tuition yet or not."

If he hadn't paid it, she really didn't want to think about what that might mean, the fight that would incur.

He patted her on the ass. "Then get your laptop and hop to it. I'll make us breakfast."

She retrieved it from downstairs and set it on the coffee table. Opening it, she logged on before going to get herself a cup of coffee from the kitchen.

"So are you really okay about last night?" he asked.

"I won't deny I was nervous, but you seem to have a way of distracting me so I don't notice it."

"I know. I'm tricky like that."

She grinned. "Yes, you are." She poured herself a cup of coffee and realized for the first time that morning how light her soul felt.

"And do you know what I'm going to do with you today?" he murmured in her ear.

"I can only hope."

He set her coffee mug down on the counter and wrapped his arms around her again. "I'm going to..." His voice trailed off and didn't continue.

She giggled. "To what? Keep me in suspense?"

His voice sounded different, guarded, when he finally spoke again. "Mal, what's up with your laptop?"

"Huh?" She looked over the counter, to where it sat on the coffee table in the living room area. "What do you mean?"

He let go of her and circled around the counter. "The webcam's on. The light's blue."

Now she saw it.

"Oh, fuck!" She followed him around as he sat down in front of it and started working on it. Then, he slammed the cover shut. "How long has it been doing that?"

"I hadn't ever noticed it before!" But there'd been plenty of times it'd sat on her dresser, open, or on the coffee table, or...

She swallowed hard. "Shit."

"How long have you had it?"

"Two years. My uncle got it for me for school when I needed an upgrade." She jumped onto his train of thought. "My uncle is a moron, a complete IT idiot. He can barely work the coffeemaker, for chrissake. There's lots of ways to get malware."

"You have pretty good antivirus software. And you keep it up to date."

"He's a techno-idiot."

"Any idiot can pay someone to install malware for them."

"Fuck."

"I need to call Tony." Kel got up and raced for his cell phone.

* * * *

So much for their sexy Sunday.

After eating, they showered, dressed, and headed to Tony and Shayla's, with Mal's laptop and charger in the backseat. Kel didn't know what the hell was going on, but something deep in his gut told him Mal's uncle was behind it. That was confirmed when Tony, after putting a piece of masking tape over the webcam, powered the laptop up and started working on it.

"You want the good news or the bad news?" he finally announced.

"Bad," he and Mal both said.

"Looking at the file dates, whoever did this installed it when the computer was new. This isn't some random malware you picked up surfing the Internet. It was deliberately installed when the computer was purchased, or shortly thereafter."

"That's the bad news?" Kel asked. Actually, it confirmed his suspicions.

"Well, there's worse news."

"Crap," she muttered.

"It's also got a key logger program, and has been sending copies of files offsite."

"Can you figure out where?"

"Done. It's been e-mailing them to a N-mail user. sweaversrq@nmail.link Sound familiar?"

"Son of a bitch," she said. "My uncle?"

"It gets better," Tony warned.

"And by better, you mean worse," she said.

"Yep. A large batch of image files were sent a couple of weeks ago. Your shoot with Jaymzon."

She groaned, dropping her head into her hands. "Fuck. Me."

"Can you scrub the computer?" Kel asked.

"Yeah, but it can't call back anything that already went out. When I get it scrubbed, you need to go in and change all your passwords to everything. Once he realizes the honeypot's dried up, no telling what he'll do. What's going on with all that, anyway?"

"Ed's still gathering info," Kel said.

The attorney didn't want to get Mallory's hopes up, but he'd confided in Kel that it looked like the uncle might be sitting on a pile of money, if Saul hadn't embezzled it from the trust. That her parents had set up a trust for her in their will, and her grandfather had left her his entire estate as a trust, comprised of several millions of dollars, as well as property, cutting Saul out in the process. Ed was hoping to get the case to a point he could file an official motion against the uncle within a week or two to force him to comply with the way the trusts were laid out.

"So the fucker has proof of what she's been doing?" Kel asked Tony. "Can you tell if he's been perving on her through the cam?"

"Yeah, there were some screenshots here and here, but they mostly look like they were taken by accident when the camera came on. There was one of you from this morning, leaning in and looking at the webcam."

"Then he knows."

"Or soon will," Tony confirmed. "When he can't access her computer or get log files anymore, he'll know it's been discovered. Frankly, I would suggest completely wiping the computer and starting over."

"I need to get new backups of my stuff," Mallory said.

"I can do that for you. But I wouldn't trust a system restore on this machine because the malware might be embedded in it or one of the partitions. Only a full wipe and reinstall will take care of that."

"Do what you need to, Tony," Kel said. "I really appreciate this."

She looked absolutely miserable on the ride home. "That fucking asshole," she said. "He's still a pain in my ass, and I don't even live there anymore."

Her weekly allowances were still being deposited. Ed had posed to Kel that it was likely a stipulation in the trust agreements, and her uncle maybe didn't want to press his luck and risk running afoul of any explicit trust guidelines he was supposed to adhere to as the executor. Although, there was a better than good chance her uncle was already in violation by not turning the trusts over to her.

Kel also hoped it meant the bulk of the money was still there, not missing. That the uncle was simply trying to force her to go to grad school as a way to bypass the trustee issue and live off her for a while longer, maybe by not having to pay his own living expenses or something. Her car and the house were both owned by the trust, free and clear.

Kel reached across the seat and took her hand. "We'll face this together. Remember, I don't give a shit if he tries to out me or not. I'm out. There's nothing he can do to us if we don't let him."

"He could make life miserable for our friends."

"And you saw how Tilly reacted to that. I strongly suspect he's only using that as a threat, that he won't really do it."

He hoped. Then again, there were people assholish and selfish enough out there who didn't care how many lives they ruined in the process.

He prayed Saul wasn't one of them.

Although considering some of their friends, if Saul dared fuck with them he might wish he'd never been born by the time they finished with him.

* * * *

Kel tried to distract Mallory the rest of the day, but knew this latest development had hit her hard emotionally. Instead, they curled up in front of the TV and enjoyed a zombie marathon.

The next afternoon, Mallory was out at work when someone knocked on Kel's office door. He opened it to find a process server standing there.

"Mallory Ann Weaver?" the guy asked.

"Seriously? Dude. Do I look like a Mallory Ann to you, buddy?"

"Does she live here?"

"Yes."

He made Kel sign for it. After locking the door behind the guy, Kel ripped the envelope open and read the contents.

An emergency competency hearing, to be held first thing Wednesday morning.

Fuck.

His first call was to Ed. Kel used his iPad to scan the documents and e-mail them to the attorney, who called him back minutes later.

"Is this a joke? It's a joke, right? The guy thinks he's going to win based on *this* bullshit?" Ed laughed. "I wonder what cut-rate paralegal he's got helping him."

"I haven't told her yet. The papers just came. What do I tell her?"

"The truth, that we're going to kick his ass. Did you look to see who the judge is?"

He hadn't paid attention to that. Then...

Kel burst out laughing. "No shit?"

"No shit. Can you bring her in here tomorrow morning at eight to go over this?"

"Yeah."

"Meanwhile, it's very important to make sure she does not contact her uncle. Tie her up if you have to, but don't let her—or anyone else for that matter, like Tilly—go after the uncle. I'll wipe him up in court. I have enough of the trust documentation I can get a ruling on the executorship. I'll be filing an emergency countermotion this afternoon to be heard at the same time. Tell her not to freak out."

"Not going to be easy."

"I'm sure you have your ways."

Kel hung up and reread the papers. Her uncle was trying to have her declared mentally incompetent, make sure the control of the trusts remained with him, and have himself appointed as her custodian and guardian for all matters.

Asshole.

If the man was that desperate, Kel could only imagine the world of hurt he was in to think this ploy would work.

He drove over to the consignment shop. Mal's expression darkened when he walked in.

"What's going on?" she immediately asked. "What's wrong?"

"Are you alone?"

"My boss is here."

"Ask for a quick break." He held up the papers. "It's important."

He watched Mal's face as she read through them. "That son of a bitch!" she screamed.

"Shh." He didn't think there were any customers out front, but her yell of outrage could easily be heard from where they stood in the back room. "I already talked to Ed. We're meeting with him in the morning and he's filing a countermotion."

"I…I just…I have no words for how pissed off I feel right now."

"I know. But you cannot contact him at all. Promise me."

She glared at him.

"*Promise* me."

"Fine." She shoved the papers at him. "What am I supposed to do until then?"

"Try not to think about it."

"*Really?*"

He pulled her in for a hug. "Do you trust me?"

She let out a long, sad-sounding sigh. "Yes," she whispered.

He kissed the top of her head. "Then try not to think about it."

"Easier said than done."

"Ed's good. This is the turning point your case needed. Your uncle just screwed up in a big, big way. This is a good thing, believe it or not."

Another sigh. "I believe you. I just don't believe this whole situation."

"I know."

"Can I call Tilly?"

"*I'll* call Tilly. After I call Landry and Cris and warn them to sit on her so she doesn't go kill your uncle."

"I never want to get on her bad side. I'm glad she's our friend."

"Believe me, so am I. She's scary."

"You've got *that* right. But I love her."

"So do I, sweetheart. And because she was there for you that night when we got you moved out, I'll be forever grateful to her for protecting you until I got there."

"I think she was hoping my uncle would put his hands on her or me."

"I know she was. Landry said she was disappointed she didn't get to punch the guy."

"Why is he being like this?"

"Some people are just born assholes," he told her. "There's no explaining it. They just are."

Chapter Twenty-Three

Wednesday morning, with Kel on one side of her, Tilly on the other, and Chelbie and Seth following behind them, Mallory nervously trailed Ed Payne into the waiting area outside the judge's chambers while ignoring her uncle's icy glare.

The attorney had warned her not to speak unless she was asked a direct question by the judge or one of the attorneys, and to not respond to any snarky comments her uncle might sling her way. Tilly, Kel, Chelbie, and Seth couldn't go in with her, because they might be called as witnesses if things got that far.

The night before, at Kel's urging and with him holding her hand, Mal had reached out and called her Aunt Susan, the first time she'd talked to her in over a year.

And when Mallory revealed everything to her aunt, an enlightening conversation had ensued.

Such as her aunt admitting one of the reasons she'd divorced Saul was because of this exact situation. That he'd wanted them to live off the trust fund monies and squirrel their money away. Not squander the trust funds, but that if they played things right, they would be able to save up money to ensure their own retirement while the trust fund paid for their living expenses, vehicles, all of that. All they'd have to do was make sure Mallory went to grad school so they could milk it as long as possible before they had to hand over control to her.

When Susan had threatened to report what he was doing, he'd threatened in return to file a police report against her, alleging she'd been sexually abusing Mallory.

As a teacher, that was something she couldn't afford to have on her record, even once she'd been exonerated. It didn't matter that, at the time, Mallory had been old enough the courts and police would believe her. Saul had threatened to destroy her reputation if she didn't just walk away.

All that fueled Mallory's hatred of the man and her desire to cut him out of her life once and for all. He wasn't family.

Family didn't do that kind of bullshit to people they loved.

Family was there to support you, to love you, to boost you up, to help you out.

Saul had never been family. Not really.

Not in the ways that truly mattered.

Once the bailiff closed the door and called the session into order, the judge entered and took his place behind his desk. "You may be seated." He looked over the file in front of him. "Emergency competency motion, I see, and countermotions." He looked at her uncle's attorney and started asking questions.

Mallory forced herself to sit there, silent, hands tightly clasped together in her lap and pretending it was Kel's fingers around hers as she squeezed.

After several minutes of summation and pontificating by her uncle's attorney, the judge focused on her and her attorney. "Counselor, your response? I have a feeling I already understand this case, but I want to hear everything before I enter my findings."

"Your Honor, what the plaintiff hasn't mentioned is the value of the trusts that are at stake. You have the exhibits in the file of the financials. Saul Weaver has engaged in a pattern of behavior over the years to conceal the existence of a significant amount of money and property from Miss Weaver, both inherited by her upon the death of her parents, and the estate left to her upon the death of Saul Weaver's father, her paternal grandfather. Saul Weaver only benefitted from this as long as he was the executor of the trusts. Which was as long as Miss Weaver was in school and agreed to allow him to remain the executor. She has already stated her intent to enter the workforce instead of attending graduate school, and by all rights, the control of the trusts should have been handed over to her upon her eighteenth birthday. However, Saul Weaver abused his position as executor by not revealing all the details or offering her the option to take the responsibilities over for herself when she turned eighteen, and by refusing all attempts on her part to gain information about the trusts. Also, he gave her a laptop computer that he used to illegally spy on her without her permission…"

She tuned it out. She didn't want to focus on the words. She only wanted to get out of there and back into the comfort of Kel's arms. This was like having to deal with the death of her parents all over again, the emergency custody hearing, the probate, all of it bringing back horrible memories and feelings that had been the start of her living nightmare.

The judge looked at her uncle's attorney. "What is the basis of your claim about her incompetency?"

"Miss Weaver has been engaging in extremely risky behavior, including putting her health and welfare in jeopardy to make pornography."

The judge's eyebrows went up. "Pornography?"

"Yes. She—"

"Hold on a second, counselor," the judge said. "Is Miss Weaver legally an adult?"

"Well, yes, but—"

"And has she ever faced questions about her competency in the past?"

"No, but—"

"So the entire basis of your argument is that her uncle wants to hold the reins of an estate that legally should have been handed over to her nearly five years ago because she's been taking dirty pictures?"

She felt hope swell in her when her attorney coughed, masking what suspiciously sounded like laughter.

"You don't understand!" her uncle said. "She's been letting some guy tie her up and take pictures of her!"

The judge's eyebrow went up again and he addressed her directly. "Miss Weaver, are you at any time being forced against your will to take the pictures?"

"No, your Honor," she said. "I wanted to." She glared at her uncle. "And I needed the money. He always refused to tell me what was in the trust."

The judge went back to her uncle's attorney. "Do you have statements from mental health professionals attesting to her incapacity?"

The attorney's face went redder. "No, but—"

"Here's how I see it," the judge said, closing the file and resting his hand on it, patting it as he spoke. "I see there is a considerable amount of money and property at stake here. Money and property that should have, legally and by the very guidelines of the trust, been handed over to Miss Weaver by your client years ago. Yes, there are stipulations about her attending school. But it would seem your client has taken advantage of those stipulations and twisted them around to make it advantageous for him by not offering her the opportunity to take control of the trusts for herself.

"So here's what I'm going to do. Plaintiff's motion is denied in full, with prejudice. And Plaintiff is responsible for paying Miss Weaver's attorney and court fees out of his own pocket, not that of the trust funds. Furthermore, I am ordering that all assets of the trusts, and paperwork relating to them, be immediately handed over to Miss Weaver. As in today, and the Plaintiff's access to any and all banking or other financial or retirement accounts be immediately revoked. If any evidence shows the Plaintiff diverted funds from the trusts for his own use, those will be immediately returned to the trust or the Plaintiff will be found in contempt of court and jailed."

The judge glared at Saul. "You're damn lucky she's not pressing charges against you for the computer."

The judge looked at her attorney. "Am I correct in my reading that the Plaintiff and Respondent's residence is an asset of the trust?"

"You are, your Honor."

He nodded. "Miss Weaver, do you want your uncle out of the house? I can enter a finding to that effect as well."

When she realized both the judge and her attorney were waiting on her for an answer, she nodded. "Yes, your Honor." She faced her uncle, staring him down. "I want him out of *my* house. Today."

"So ordered," the judge said. "I'm also entering an order of protection for Miss Weaver. Your client is ordered to immediately vacate the premises, and he has until noon tomorrow to remove his belongings from the home, and he'd better have a deputy with him when he does it. He is no longer allowed unsupervised contact with Miss Weaver."

He pointed a finger at her uncle. "I'm halfway tempted to have you thrown in jail for contempt of court, because, technically, you are. The probate courts in New Jersey and North Dakota entered orders regarding the trusts and you have violated them. Lucky for you, she isn't asking for a contempt finding." He glanced at her attorney. "Is she?" She thought the judge almost sounded hopeful.

Her attorney gave up trying not to smile. "No, your Honor. She only wants the trusts and all their assets turned over to her, and her uncle immediately removed from the home."

"So ordered. Counsel for respondent, you write the final order. I want it on my desk so I can sign it by end of business today. If the assets are not transferred immediately to Miss Weaver, I will issue a bench warrant for Saul Weaver's arrest by eight o'clock tomorrow morning." He looked at her uncle. "Do you understand me, Mr. Weaver?"

She thought her uncle was going to argue, but his attorney spoke up. "Yes, your Honor. Clearly."

When they finished and the judge left the room, her attorney briefly conferred with her uncle's attorney. All the while, her uncle sat there, glaring at her.

This time, she glared back.

When he finally looked away first, she couldn't help herself. "Hey, doucheball."

Her uncle flinched and turned back at the sound of her voice.

She flipped him a bird. "I talked to Aunt Susan last night. She told me what you did. If your shit isn't out of my house by noon tomorrow, it'll be out at the curb, and on fire. You ever set foot on my property again, I'll have your ass thrown in jail."

Her attorney rested a hand on her shoulder, holding her back as her uncle's attorney practically dragged the man out the door. Then they followed, gathering up Kel, Tilly, Chelbie, and Seth from the waiting room.

She practically fell into Kel's arms, eyes closed, listening as her attorney gleefully filled them in about what happened.

"Let me make some calls real fast," Seth said. "I want people at the house now, in case he tries any bullshit, like steal stuff, or trash it, or set fire to it." He stepped out into the hallway.

Kel smiled down at her. "See? Told you it'd be okay."

"I know. It's just hard to believe it was that easy. All these years I spent fighting him, I never believed it'd be this simple to take him down and get the truth."

Chelbie tapped her on the shoulder and got a hug from her, too. "Hey, if you'd actually, you know, *listened* to me all those times I tried to get you to do this earlier, it would have been done by now."

"I'm sorry. You were right."

"Yay!" Chelbie cheered. "Y'all heard it. She said I was right!"

"Well," Tilly said, cracking her knuckles, "I for one plan on spending the rest of today and tonight and tomorrow morning over at the house. Let the guy try to cause trouble. I *dare* him," she added in a dark and threatening tone.

"We don't need you in jail," Kel playfully said.

She grinned. "Hey, no body, no jail."

"Tilly," Ed warned. "Landry told me I'm not allowed to let you get arrested."

She rolled her eyes. "*Fine*," she huffed. "No one ever lets me have any fun." She stepped in and hugged Mallory. "Congratulations, sweetie. We all knew this would work out in your favor."

A prickle of tears threatened. "It feels like I really have a family again," she said.

Kel slipped his arm around her waist and pulled her tightly against her side. "That's because you *do*. We *are* your family."

"Yeah, and we don't want you for your money, either," Chelbie said.

"I hate to break this up," her attorney said, "but I have to run back to the office and get this ready for the judge ASAP. Meet me there at five this afternoon. That's when his attorney will turn everything over."

"Is it that easy?" Kel asked.

"Well, there will be more paperwork, I'm sure. But the court order will override and bulldoze through any issues that might crop up. And I plan on having that ready for the judge's signature in less than an hour, so I can send copies to the bank and get Saul off the accounts. I'll rework all the trust papers to take him off everything and we'll file all that in the next couple of days. Meanwhile, the emergency court order will hold us over and let us get started."

"I feel like lunch," Kel said, smiling down at her. "Let's go celebrate before we finish this day."

Seth returned. "Okay. I've got four guys on their way to the house now, with explicit orders not to let the uncle in if he shows up, unless he has a deputy."

"Aw," Kel said. "We were going to get lunch."

"Oh, we absolutely will go get lunch," Seth said. "But let's run by the house first and drop a key off so they can wait inside in the AC. And we'll bring them back lunch."

Mallory's vision blurred as the tears broke through again. "You have no idea how grateful I am to all of you for your help."

Seth laughed and hugged her. Then he whispered, "Hey, this was a slam dunk. Judge Donnelly is a friend of mine. Pat married me and Leah. He doesn't get out to the club, but he's in the lifestyle. We didn't want to say anything to you before, but there were no doubts you would win this."

Her tears transformed to laughter as Seth stepped back. He wore a playful grin.

"What?" Kel asked, curious and looking from Seth to her.

Seth shook his head. "Tell you later, bro. Let's get moving."

Chapter Twenty-Four

With the papers signed and filed, they went out for a celebration dinner at Sigalo's with their friends. Kel was pleased to see the worry had lifted from Mal's face, but he was eager to get her home, and alone.

It was nearly eleven that night when Kel and Mallory returned to the apartment.

"Straight to bed," he ordered. "No passing go, no collecting two hundred dollars."

"What about passing a bathroom?"

He swatted her on the ass. "Hurry. I'm horny and want to do a little celebratory fucking."

"Yes, Sir."

He was naked and lying on his back, camera in hand, a condom pouch next to him, and his cock hard and ready when she walked into the room. He pointed at his cock. "Start sucking, baby."

She stripped on her way to the bed, naked by the time she climbed up onto the mattress and between his legs. Smiling at him, she slowly picked up and opened the condom pouch. He photographed her as she did, these pictures strictly for his own pleasure. He wanted to document this night, the victorious, sexy glow radiating from her as she rolled the condom down his shaft and knelt, ready and waiting.

He reached down with one hand and fisted her hair, the other working the camera. "Deep, baby," he said. "Just a little. Then I want you to ride me."

She kept her eyes on him, the blue like crystals in his camera, as she slowly engulfed his shaft with her mouth.

Oh, she was good. So fucking good.

After a few minutes, and a few more pictures, he knew he'd blow if he didn't get his cock into her. He tugged on her hair, pulling her off his cock.

"Mount and ride, sweetheart," he said, the camera focused on her face.

She did, letting out a soft moan as she settled on top of his cock.

"Play with yourself," he hoarsely said. "Let me watch you."

She did, reaching down and finding her clit, slowly massaging it as she rocked on his cock.

"I'm going to have to pierce your nipples," he said, reaching up and twisting one, then the other. "And your clit hood. I think you'd look gorgeous all blinged out for me."

She smiled, sexy, seductive, the subby glaze already in her face. "Whatever Sir wants me to do."

"Do you want to do it?"

"I want to play in the shadows with you."

He put the camera aside and grabbed her, flipping her onto her back so he could press her thighs into her chest. He reached around and grabbed her ass with his hands, nails digging in, squeezing until she gasped.

"I play deep in the shadows, sweetheart. In the darkness. And I have a lot of fun there. And if you want to play with me there, I'll be glad to have you. But don't you dare do anything only because I want you to. It's only fun for me if you want me to do it to you."

"I do," she said.

He slowed, sitting up and pulling her legs around him so he could reach down and grab her breasts. "Hands over your head," he ordered.

She immediately complied.

He pinched her nipples, tweaking them, tugging on them, until she winced and cried out again, making his cock throb inside her pussy.

"That's nothing. That's full daylight," he said. "I want to do a corset lacing up your back around needles I've placed there myself," he said. "I want to pierce your nipples with my own hands, place my rings there, so you remember who owns you every time they rub against something."

He reached down between her legs and found her clit, pinching it not quite as hard as her nipples, but still rough. "You're going to get to the point where pain and pleasure blend into one, and you crave both of them, together. Maybe even get you to the point where pain makes you come. The brain is a funny thing, easily trainable if you know what you're doing."

He eased up on her clit, rolling it between his fingers now, making her gasp and moan in pleasure. "And when I want you to come for me, you will come for me, or I'll keep trying until you do."

He reached up to her breasts with his other hand, squeezing them, back and forth, pinching her nipples.

Then she came, her moans music to his soul. He pinched her nipple, hard, her moan turning into a whine and back again to a moan as he kept her coming, loving that her body responded to him so easily.

She was perfect. Perfect for him, and perfect in his eyes.

Gorgeous.

When he knew she'd finished, he braced his arms against the bed and started fucking her. "Look at me, baby."

She forced her eyes open. He grinned, her crazed, glazed, subby look exactly what he wanted to see.

"There's My girl," he said, feeling his release growing closer, his balls drawing up tight, ready, wanting to explode.

Reaching down, he grabbed her thighs and squeezed, hard, her cries driving him over the edge and blasting his orgasm straight from his balls up his spine and to his brain, until he collapsed on her, winded.

She wrapped her arms around him, holding him tightly.

"I'll always want to play with *You*, Sir. Wherever you want to play with me. I'll always follow you."

He closed his eyes, inhaling the scent of their lovemaking, the scent of her.

"I hope so, sweetheart," he said. "I really, really do."

Chapter Twenty-Five

It felt weird in a good way to wake up in her own bedroom and snuggled up against Kel.

Maybe I finally caught a break in my life.

When she started to feel the slightest bit badly about having booted her uncle out, she did what everyone else had told her to do, which was to remember how he would have kept her dependent upon him as long as he could have, as long as the money held out.

Living her own life never would have happened. He wouldn't have allowed it. He was too busy sponging off her while hoarding his own money.

Bastard.

Three weeks later, it still didn't feel real. She was about to start her next semester at Ringling. Kel, Seth, Leah, and Ed were working with her to teach her what she needed to know about investing.

And she and Kel now lived in the house instead of the apartment. She hadn't worked herself up to move into the master bedroom there yet, wanting time to mentally decompress and get used to her freedom before making that change.

Besides, as long as she had Kel, she didn't care what bed or bedroom she was in, as long as he shared it with her.

He rolled over and hooked an arm around her, snuggling close against her ass. "Where you think you're going?"

She giggled. "Nowhere."

"Damn straight." He nibbled on the top of her shoulder, working his way down to the fleshy part of her upper arm before biting. That was his morning routine, that, somewhere, he marked her. Sometimes with his teeth...

She pleasantly shivered, feeling her pussy grow wet.

Sometimes he used a blade, or needles. Both her nipples were now pierced with captive bead rings, and he was talking about getting her a vertical clit hood piercing. He'd pierced her nipples himself, but he was trying to decide whether or not to take her to a friend of his to have her clit pierced.

That way, he could tie her down and photograph it being done.

He nuzzled the back of her neck. "I was thinking about something."

"Yesss?"

"Do you still want to be collared to me?"

She turned in his arms to face him. "Really?"

He nodded. "Really."

"Yes, Sir."

"I meant it when I say I don't take it lightly. It's not a case of you get pissed off at me, you throw the collar at me and then a couple of hours later you want it back. You still belong to me. If you ever decide you don't want that, you have to ask me to uncollar you. I'll never force you to be with me, but I won't play games."

She arched an eyebrow at him.

"Games of the not-fun kind," he clarified.

"Yes, Sir," she said. "I want to wear your collar."

He rolled her onto her back, grabbing her hands and pinning them over her head with one hand, while he easily fed his hard cock into her pussy with the other. She was already wet for him. Their morning routine always left her wet, frustratingly so if they didn't have time for him to make her come after leaving his mark on her.

She let out a soft moan at the feel of his cock inside her. No more condoms, they were fluid bonded to each other and her birth control pills worked.

Holla!

He slowly fucked her, building her up, knowing her body so well already. "Give me what I want," he whispered. "Give me what's mine." He nuzzled his face between her breasts, nipping at them, along the sides and avoiding her still-tender nipples. "Give it to me," he sternly commanded.

He bit down on the inside of her left breast, and that did it. Her orgasm crested, exploding. Kel sped up his strokes, fucking her hard, fast, driving his cock deep into her the way she loved. Craved.

Needed.

"Good girl," he grunted before finally finishing with her, filling her.

Marking her inside as well as out.

As they caught their breaths, he released her wrists, kissing first one, then the other, before rolling onto his side and taking her with him.

"So, Saturday?" he asked, catching her by surprise.

"Huh?"

He laughed. "Collaring on Saturday?"

"Yes, sorry. You have a habit of scrambling my brain."

"I think you mean I *love* scrambling your brain." He touched his index finger to the center of her forehead. "Those little synapses of yours are probably spelling out K-E-L now."

She giggled. He might have a dark side that liked to play in the shadows, but dammit, he was a lot of fun, too. Had a silly side she knew most people never saw. "Yes, Sir. I hope so."

He nuzzled noses with her. "Okay. So, Saturday. I'll talk with Loren and the gang and make the arrangements." He smiled. "And we're going shopping."

* * * *

Mallory forced herself to stand still while Chelbie and Tilly worked on tightening the corset Kel had driven her all the way to Ft. Lauderdale to buy that past Wednesday.

"Girl, you've got titillating ta-tas," Tilly teased. "Your man will be drooling when he watches you walk down the aisle."

Mallory giggled. "Thank you, ma'am."

"Aw, you don't have to ma'am me, kiddo," she said. "I'm just really happy for the two of you."

"About time you got your happily ever after," Chelbie said. "You of all people deserve it."

She felt one of the women tie the laces off. "Okay," Tilly said. "There you go. Wiggle around and let me know how that feels."

Mallory turned and looked in the mirror, gasping as she did. "I have a shape!" The gorgeous royal blue corset had tamed her convex midsection into hourglass curves.

Tilly snorted. "You're just now noticing that? Seriously, sweetie, you're gorgeous." She rested her hands on Mallory's shoulders and met her gaze in the mirror. "So what if you're not a twig? You're a reader. Do you like all books? No. Some people like short stories, and some people like epics. You're epic."

Chelbie laughed. "She is epic. Thank you for saying that. I've been trying to convince her of that as long as I've known her."

Mallory turned to face the two women again. "Am I making a mistake?"

Tilly's serious face returned. She took Mallory's hands in hers. "What do you feel for him?"

"I love him."

"Then it's not a mistake."

"But it happened so fast. I mean, look what happened to Abbey and how long they were together." Tilly's good friend had just been dumped by her boyfriend of several years, and right before she had to have back surgery for an injury.

"So? I knew Landry less than a month when I married him."

"Yeah, but that was totally different. And you were older than I am. Abbey and her ex were together how long?"

"Again, so? Totally different situation. He is a selfish fucktard who dumped her when she needed him the most just because she couldn't be dominant enough for him. Forget about that. This is *your* life we're talking about. Look at everything you've accomplished in a short amount of time. You are your own person. It's time for you to follow your heart and do what makes you happy. Life is damn short, and you have had your fill of heartache. Time for you to get the happiness part of it for a change. You do not strike me as the airheaded, do-things-on-a-whim kind of woman. And Kel is a good guy. I've never met anyone except his batcrap crazy ex who says otherwise."

Chelbie spoke up. "Why do you think this is a mistake?" she asked Mallory.

"I don't. I mean, I don't think it is, but what if it is?"

Chelbie's grin lit her face. "Quit trying to punish yourself. Do you honestly think I'd let you do this if I thought this was a mistake? If you'll recall, I was the one cautioning you in the beginning when you moved into his place. But I can see a light in you that you've never had before. He has to be good for you. You know I'd never lie to you."

That pulled Mallory up short. No, of all her friends, she could count on Chelbie to be brutally honest when need be.

"I'm scared," she whispered.

"Why?" the other two women asked.

"What if I disappoint him?"

Tilly enveloped her in her arms. "Stop it. Quit thinking about what might go wrong and start thinking about what might go right. You're not going to disappoint him unless you keep beating yourself up. You know how he feels about that and rightfully so. You guys make magic together."

Tilly stepped back. "Loren is going to be wondering where the hell we are if we don't get out there pretty soon. I want to get this started before Gilo figures out what's going on, shows up, and I have to kill the son of a bitch for good."

"I heard Shayla stocked up on duct tape for you," Chelbie said.

"I love that woman."

They cleared out of the bathroom and returned to the playspace. Mallory felt her face heat as she noticed several of the men doing double-takes.

Chelbie leaned in and whispered, "See? You're tenting those Doms' pants. You're gorgeous."

"I don't care about their pants. Only Kel's."

Ross walked over to join them, a smile on his face. "You look beautiful," he said, offering her his arm. "Ready?"

"Where's Kel?"

"Tony's getting him."

They passed a small group of people gathered by one of the couches when Tilly pulled up short in front of Mallory and Ross and literally took a couple of steps backward.

Thunderclouds filled Tilly's face. "What the hell are *you* doing here?" she said to a nice-looking guy in a suit who'd been talking with Abbey.

He held up his hands in a placating manner. "Calm down, Tilly," he said. "I just came from a funeral. Don't worry, I'm not going to cause trouble." He faced Mallory and gave her a slight, respectful bow. "Congratulations. You look beautiful. I hope you and Kel have many years of happiness together."

Then Mallory realized it was Gilo. She hadn't recognized him at first, his hair neatly combed instead of spiked up, no kohl eyeliner, and not dressed in his usual leather or latex garb, and no hood or mask.

Tilly's jaw opened and closed a couple of times, like she was going to say something but had been rendered speechless. Finally, she jabbed a finger in his face. "Behave yourself, or you won't walk straight ever again."

He cocked his head, arching an eyebrow at the woman in a dominant way Mallory never imagined Gilo the unrepentant SAM could ever manage. "Believe it or not, I do have boundaries. You don't give me credit for all the times I haven't said a peep during a ceremony simply because I was asked ahead of time not to."

Tilly let out something resembling a snarl. "Yeah? Well…I'm going to have my eye on you, buster."

He blew her a kiss. "I'm flattered." A playful smile filled his face.

Mallory had to fight not to snicker. She didn't want to hurt Tilly's feelings, but there was something subtly different about Gilo today.

Tilly let out one final snort and stormed away. As Ross led Mallory toward the other side of the playspace where the chairs had been set up, Mallory's focus snapped back to the purpose of the day.

During their little aside with Gilo, Kel and Tony had come in. They now stood with Loren at the front of the room.

It felt like the world faded away as Mallory's gaze locked with Kel's. Those sexy brown eyes that had a way of burrowing into the core of her soul without even trying.

Ross leaned in and whispered, "You ready?"

"I hope so."

He patted her arm as he led her through the center aisle and toward Kel.

Everyone who wasn't already seated migrated that way, settling into hushed tones as they took their places. When Mallory looked, she caught sight of Tilly glaring at Gilo, pointing at her own eyes with two fingers on her right hand, then at Gilo, and back to herself.

I've got my eyes on you.

Gilo blew Tilly another silent kiss. Then he helped Abbey, who'd been holding onto his arm for support due to her back injury, take her seat before he sat next to her.

The giggle escaped Mallory. Apparently Kel had been paying attention and leaned in to whisper in her ear. "I called him personally and invited him, but asked him to please tone it down. Tilly's already stressed to the max as it is over Abbey."

"He said he came from a funeral."

"He did. I'm surprised and very honored he made it. He's actually a pretty nice guy."

Loren called for everyone's attention. "It is without an ounce of complaining that I observe I seem to have become the de facto official for collaring ceremonies in this neck of the woods." A ripple of laughter flowed through the space. "You all know I love doing these, right? I love happy endings and hopeful beginnings. Today, we're celebrating both, and that's not a contradiction of terms. Two very deserving people are getting the happy ending they deserve, and are starting out on a new beginning together."

She motioned to Ross, who handed Mallory off to Kel before stepping aside. Kel looked down at her, his placid smile imparting hints of the evening to come. When he squeezed her hands, a pleasant shiver washed through her.

This was happening. This was real.

This wasn't a wishful fantasy.

All she had to do was step across that threshold.

"These two," Loren continued, "are coming together before you today, their friends and adopted family, to pledge themselves to each other as Master and slave. They wish for everyone to witness their vows, a public declaration of their feelings for each other."

Tony held out a small box to Kel. She couldn't see what was inside it, until he turned to face her, the solid metal slave bracelet in his hand.

"This is your collar," Kel told her. "I offer it to you with a vow to be faithful, to protect you, to care for you, and to love you forever, for as long as you choose to wear it. You will not remove it unless you've asked me to." He smiled. "Or unless the TSA makes us take it off you, whichever comes first."

A stream of laughter rippled through the audience.

He continued. "But it's yours, a constant reminder of who owns you, who owns your body. By looking at it, I want you to know that it's a signal of my love and protection, my ownership. Marking what's mine. But you have to ask me for it."

She nodded, hoping she didn't cry and ruin her makeup. "I want to wear your collar, Sir."

"Do you promise to be faithful, to protect what's mine to the best of your abilities, to serve me…" He smiled, melting her. "To be my beautiful canvas?"

"Yes, Sir. I do."

He clamped it around her right wrist, using a special hex key to tighten the almost hidden screw that kept it in place. Then he raised her wrist to his lips and kissed it. "My sweet, beautiful goddess. I love you."

"I love you, too, Sir."

"Oh, you're not done," Loren teased. She made a motion, and then Mallory realized Tony and Seth were bringing a massage table and cart over, followed by a man she'd met before but who's name she couldn't remember.

She gulped.

On the cart were piercing supplies.

Kel grinned as Tony passed a coil of rope to him. "Oh, yes," Kel said, patting the table. "Up you go."

He quickly trussed her to the table, skirt hiked up to her waist, legs spread wide. The man, who Kel reminded her his name was George, was a piercer.

Kel pointed to the sealed package holding a curved barbell with beads at either end. "Going to start you out with that. Once you heal, we'll look into switching it out to a captive bead ring to match your nipples." He grinned as Tilly held up the camera. "Oh, and she volunteered to take the pictures for me so I can hold your hands while he does it."

She looked at Tilly. "Bitch." Then she stuck her tongue out at her.

Tilly stuck her tongue out at her in return before she smiled. "That's Princess Bitch, sweetie."

Kel moved to stand at Mallory's head, his fingers tightly twined with hers. He knelt down to whisper into her ear. "Just think about always having something rubbing against your clit and your nipples, reminding you who owns them and you."

She closed her eyes as she felt George swab her clit and labia down with antiseptic. She kept herself shaved down there per Kel's orders.

Kel's lips pressed against her ear. "My cock is so fucking hard right now," he whispered. "I want to hear you cry out when it happens."

"Hold on," Tilly said. "I need to zoom in."

Kel snickered. "Don't you love having friends who are sadists?"

"Okay," Tilly said. "I'm good. Proceed."

Mallory's grip tightened on Kel's fingers.

"It's going to go quick," George said. "Don't move. I'll do the piercing first, then place the barbell. It'll be a two-stage process."

"Take a deep breath," Kel whispered in her ear.

She did.

A sharp, stabbing pain shot through her clit, making her scream. She thought a few women in the audience might have let out sympathetic yelps of their own.

"Suck it up," Tilly said, snapping away. "It'll feel better in a couple of minutes."

She felt George doing his thing down there, another pinch of pain, and then he sat back. "Done."

Already, the pain was fading. She opened her eyes, gasping for breath.

"Such a good girl," Kel whispered in her ear. "Letting everyone watch you get pierced for me."

She shivered, in the good way.

George swabbed her down again with antiseptic before Kel quickly worked to untie her. When he helped her sit up, Tilly helpfully offered the camera.

"Want to see?" She grinned.

Mal laughed. "You really are a sadist, aren't you?"

Half of the crowd standing around them, people who heard her comment, all said, "Duh."

Chapter Twenty-Six

Mallory thought Kel would play with her there at the club, but he didn't. He proudly spent the night with her holding onto his arm, or his arm draped around her, or with her sitting on his lap on one of the couches.

When it came time for the drive home, he helped her into the passenger seat. "I have to admit, living next door does have its advantages," he said.

"Yeah, but it's nice not having to listen to the music on the weekends when we don't want to."

"True."

He still worked there, in his downstairs office. But they hadn't decided what, if anything, to do with the apartment yet. They could still crash there on weekend nights after playing at the club, and had a couple of times.

Or they could retreat over there to fuck like bunnies, something the club's rules didn't allow, and then return to join their friends.

Tonight he drove them back to the house, opening her car door for her and helping her out, walking her into the house.

In the bedroom, he helped her out of the corset and skirt and knelt to examine her new piercing. They weren't supposed to do oral sex with it for a couple of weeks to give it time to heal.

Didn't mean he couldn't do other things, though.

He tied her facedown across the bed, knees bent and legs spread wide, a towel under her.

"I still owe you that promise I made about filling you all in one night," he teased, "but tonight isn't that night. However, I am going to fuck that beautiful ass of yours."

She heard him getting things ready, then the sound of him getting naked before he knelt on the bed, between her legs.

"Now then." A vibrator clicked on. She realized it was one of the egg types just before he slid it into her pussy, making her moan as it lodged itself firmly against her G-spot.

"Oh, that feels good, doesn't it?" He bit her on the ass, hard, making her cry out and her clit throb all at the same time.

Yep. Pain now made her horny.

And it made her even hornier knowing how hot it made Kel.

"That's it," he said. "Make lots of noise for me. You know I love it." He bit her other ass cheek just as hard, until she cried out.

"You will come for me tonight, with that shiny new piercing lying along your clit." Fortunately, it was just in the hood, not in the actual bundle of nerves of her clit itself.

Close enough, in the same neighborhood, to make everything down there stand up and holla.

She felt him squirt lube down the crack of her ass and the sound of him snapping on a glove. "We're going to take a shower after we're done," he said, his tone turning serious. "Because I don't want to risk any problems with your new piercing."

Frankly, she already loved the piercing. The dull throbbing ache in her clit had kept her on edge all night. All her friends who had one assured her that within a day or so she likely wouldn't have any pain at all, that it healed far faster than nipples.

And that once it fully healed, she would begin to truly appreciate the benefits of having it.

She heard the sound of him rolling a condom onto his cock before he pressed the knob against her rim. The slight pinching burn as her body stretched to accommodate him was all she needed to pitch her over the edge.

He laughed as he continued to ease his cock into her ass. "You've already started coming, haven't you?" He smacked her ass, hard, making her moan even louder.

And come even harder.

Once his cock was completely fisted inside her ass, he held still, waiting for her to catch her breath. While he did that, he raked his nails down her back and over her ass, making her moan again.

Inside her pussy, the vibrating egg happily hummed away, quickly driving her toward another orgasm. She felt him reach over for something, then came the words that always sent a thrill up her spine.

"Hold still," he said.

She could visualize the sadistic smile on his face.

The feel of the cold steel against her flesh, against her ass cheeks, as he gently traced the blade's tip around in circles, not enough to break the skin—yet—but feeling almost like a cat's claw dragging along her flesh.

"Where to put this one," he teased. "So many beautiful choices." He traced the blade up her spine, down again. Up, across the back of her shoulders, back to her ass.

He nicked her on the right ass cheek with the tip, making her cry out, her body clenching around his cock in her ass and the egg vibrating in her pussy.

"That's it, baby," he whispered. "You know what I love to hear." He nicked her left ass cheek, and that did it.

Over she went.

He chuckled, putting the blade aside as he slowly fucked her ass, drawing her release out. "That's the other sound I love to hear. The sound of you coming around my cock."

He held on to her hips, digging his nails in, making her cry out again.

It felt so good, a mix of pleasure and pain that she'd come to love and crave, the feel of his hands on her.

"Such a good girl." He picked up the knife again and gently poked her in the ass, both cheeks. "Hold very, very still. This knife is extremely sharp."

She gasped, trying not to move, not to wiggle as he poked her ass cheeks, his cock firmly wedged deep inside her. Then the tears started as they sometimes did, her brain's wiring short-circuiting as she tried to force her body to hold still against the pleasure and pain inside and out.

He laughed. "There she goes."

He set the knife aside again and started fucking her, hard, fast, one more orgasm sweeping through her from the force of his strokes, the sensation of his cock pressing the egg against her G-spot.

"Such a good girl." His body stiffened, going rigid as he took one last, hard stroke and ended up with his cock deep inside her.

He folded his body over hers, catching his breath, kissing her along her back. "Hold on." She winced as he withdrew. She heard him walk into the bathroom, the sounds of him cleaning up before he returned and untied her.

"Bath time," he said, helping her up off the bed, capturing her right wrist and kissing her where the bracelet now rested on her arm.

In the shower he bathed her, taking his time, fingers slipping across her flesh, holding her body against his as the warm water sluiced over them.

This was heaven. Or felt like it. Compared to the last several years of her life, at least.

She knew there were some who might disagree, who wouldn't understand, who would condemn her for her choices.

They could go take a flying fuck for all she cared.

"Who's *My* good girl?" he whispered in her ear.

She tipped her head back to look up into his eyes. "Me, Sir."

He smiled down at her. "Yes, you are." He nipped the side of her neck. "*My* very good girl."

They snuggled in bed, Mallory closing her eyes, her ear pressed against his chest as she listened to his heart.

"I love you, Sir," she whispered.

He nuzzled the top of her head. "I love you, too, My sweet goddess."

* * * *

The next afternoon, they drove to Kel's mom's house. Michelle Hansen lived only twenty minutes away from where Mallory's house was.

Their house was.

Yet another good reason to live there instead of the apartment.

Mal loved Kel's mom. They tried to have dinner with her at least once a week, and Michelle Hansen had insisted from the first dinner together that Mal call her "Mom."

Of course she did. It felt right.

One more member of her adopted family to complete her life.

The woman also had eagle eyes. They'd no sooner come in and hugged her than she noticed the bracelet on Mal's right wrist. "That's new," she said, admiring the rounded metal, niobium bracelet that seemed to shimmer and change colors. "Where did you get that?"

"I got it for her," Kel said, sparing Mal any explanations. He laced his fingers with Mal's. "Mom, Mal and I are living together."

She smiled. "I know, silly."

"No, not just as roommates. We're living together, permanently."

Michelle rolled her eyes. "I know." She shrugged. "I know what the two of you told me that first night you brought her to dinner," she said, "but I could see it in you both even then. There was a magnetic attraction between you two. It's only gotten stronger the longer you've been together. I suspected you weren't lying to me then, that you were just roommates. I knew it was only a matter of time before you two became an item. And I couldn't be happier for you."

"Thanks, Mom." Kel hugged her. "I love her."

"Good." She hugged Mallory. "You love him?"

"Very much, Mom."

"Good. Now, let's go eat and quit talking about the obvious." The two little dogs danced around their feet, begging for attention. Kel reached down and scooped one of them up, loving on him before doing it to the other one.

They hadn't talked about children yet. Mallory wasn't even sure if she wanted kids. Kel hadn't mentioned it, but she suspected that, like her, he wasn't in any rush to make that decision.

They were still having too much fun dancing among the shadows with each other, exploring those dark places where she loved spending time with him.

Always with him.

When they were on their way home later, she held his hand. "I hoped she'd take it well, but that went even better than I thought it would."

He smiled. "I love my mom. I'm glad she really likes you."

"I miss my parents," she softly said. "I hated it when Saul and Aunt Susan divorced. I wish I'd fought him back then and tried to go with her."

"He wouldn't have let you," Kel said. "Ed said it, too. You're just lucky he was a stingy fuck with your money as well as his." Saul had nearly five hundred thousand dollars of his own money saved up in an account.

Which had been frozen by court order pending the outcome of their litigation.

Ed had gone after Saul, suing him to recoup improperly billed expenses and his monthly trust executor management fee. The case was winding its way through court, but Ed was pretty sure they'd have no problems getting a judge to see things her way.

And she'd bought herself a brand-new laptop.

With *her* money.

She closed her eyes and settled back in the seat, peace washing through her. "Thank you," she said.

"For what, sweetheart?"

"For showing me the shadows."

He squeezed her hand. "Thank you for wanting to play in them with me."

Chapter Twenty-Seven

"So what do you think?" Kel asked her.

She leaned in, arms circling him as her chin came to rest on his shoulder. On the screen he had his shopping cart displayed.

Containing several different colors of rope. Among them, pink, emerald green, and a royal blue a different shade than the rope he already had.

She smiled. "I like them."

"I think they'll look good against your skin tones and with your hair." He turned and kissed her. "And I can't wait to see how you look trussed up in them."

Her heart fluttered. Everything about him could do that to her. His voice, his knowing glances, the way his long, lithe fingers stepped across a keyboard, the way they stepped across her flesh. "Thank you, Sir."

"My pleasure, believe me. Are we still meeting up with Chelbie this evening?"

She'd almost forgotten. "Oh! Yeah. Sorry." She wanted to stay in the habit of walking with her friend at least once a week. She'd added pool walking two days a week at the Y to her schedule as well. The weight wasn't coming off as quickly as she'd hoped it would, but she had noticed her stamina had improved.

Since Kel wasn't complaining, she guessed she shouldn't, either.

Progress, not perfection.

After nearly eight months together, he seemed to be as into her as he was when they first finally got together.

He reached up and touched her lips. "You know I don't care about your weight, right?"

"That's spooky."

"You get this look in your eyes when you're thinking about it. Stop it. Seriously. I want you to be healthy. We have a long life together ahead of us. I fell in love with your brain and your personality. The beautiful package they came wrapped in was a bonus, not a requirement." He turned his chair around, encircling her in his arms and looking up at her. "I don't care what you weigh, as long as you never stop being the gorgeous person I fell in love with."

"I want to make you proud of me."

"I *am* proud of you." He stood, holding her against him. "Do you think I would have collared you in front of everyone if I wasn't?"

With her face pressed against his chest, she felt his heart beating. The comforting feel of his body, his scent, it all took her to a gentle, loving place in her mind where she could shove the rest of the world aside and just *be*, there, with him.

"And I was thinking," he said.

"Yeah?"

"We need to decide on a date."

She tipped her head up to meet his gaze. "What?"

His expression was all serious. "A wedding date. That collar means more to me than a piece of paper, but unfortunately, it does nothing to protect either of us in the eyes of the law. I want you to be my wife, not just my slave."

Her throat went dry. "You do?"

"Well, of course." He frowned. "I thought I made the whole 'forever' concept fairly clear at our collaring ceremony."

"I... You did, I... I mean..." Her mouth snapped shut. "Okay."

A sexy smile curved his lips. "You *do* want to marry me, don't you?"

She nodded, fast and hard.

"Okay. Just checking. You sounded a little shocked." His smile faded. "And we'll go to Ed and do everything right. Set up a pre-nup to protect you and me both, so you know I'm not after anything. That we're both doing this because we want to be together and for no other reason."

She nodded. She knew he wasn't after the estate. Just like he knew she wasn't after his money, either.

Unlike her uncle, Kel had never lied to her, never had any ulterior motives.

What she saw was what she got.

And she loved every bit about him. The light, the dark, the shadows.

Everything.

"Can we invite Gilo?" she asked.

He snorted. "Why?"

She shrugged. "He didn't get to crash our collaring. I feel kind of bad about that."

Kel laughed. "You're serious."

"Yeah. I mean, I appreciate his consideration at our collaring. But..." She shrugged. "Kind of puts us up there in a pretty decent group of people, you know? Good luck kind of thing."

He stared down at her. "Really?"

"Yeah." The truth was she'd quickly come to like Gilo, especially the more she'd learned about him. Most people hadn't seen the saner side of the SAM, his true nature. All they knew about him was the jokester from the club.

"Okay. Yeah, we can have him there. I'm guessing that means you want to have the wedding at the club?"

"Yeah." She snuggled more tightly against him. "Yeah, I do. After all, they're my adopted family. It's where you and I met. And it's where I feel most at home."

He nuzzled the top of her head. "Then that's what we'll do."

She closed her eyes and breathed in deeply. "Thank you. What about your mom?"

"I'll have a talk with her. Either she'll want to be there, or she won't. Her choice, but it's our life."

"Okay." It felt so good to be able to let go like that, to let him make the hard decisions and know he had no problem doing it. Taking charge.

Even better, that she trusted him enough to let him make them.

"Tomorrow," he said. "I want to head to the paint store."

Her eyes popped open. "Why?"

He motioned around them, at the stark, white walls of the house. "Isn't it time we make this *your* home? Take over the master bedroom? I know you haven't wanted to think about that, and I didn't want to push you. But I think it's time you either claim the house, or think about selling it and we buy something you feel comfortable in. Something you can make into your home."

She was just so happy to have her uncle out of her life, to discover she had a lot more money in the bank than she thought, and to—duh—have Kel a permanent part of her life, that redecorating hadn't topped the list of her priorities.

"I think you mean *our* home," she softly said.

He kissed her. "You're right, goddess. *Our* home."

THE END

WWW.TYMBERDALTON.COM

ABOUT THE AUTHOR

Tymber Dalton lives in the Tampa Bay region of Florida with her husband (aka "The World's Best Husband™") and too many pets. Active in the BDSM lifestyle, the two-time EPIC winner is also the bestselling author of over sixty-five books, including *The Reluctant Dom*, *The Denim Dom*, *Cardinal's Rule*, the Suncoast Society series, the Love Slave for Two series, the Triple Trouble series, the Coffeeshop Coven series, the Good Will Ghost Hunting series, the Drunk Monkeys series, and many more.

She loves to hear from readers! Please feel free to drop by her website and sign up for updates to keep abreast of the latest news, views, snarkage, and releases.

www.tymberdalton.com
www.facebook.com/tymberdalton
www.facebook.com/groups/TymbersTrybe
www.twitter.com/TymberDalton

For all titles by Tymber Dalton, please visit
www.bookstrand.com/tymber-dalton

For titles by Tymber Dalton writing as
Tessa Monroe, please visit
www.bookstrand.com/tessa-monroe

For titles by Tymber Dalton writing as
Macy Largo, please visit
www.bookstrand.com/macy-largo

For titles by Tymber Dalton writing as
Leslie Richardson, please visit
www.bookstrand.com/lesli-richardson

Siren Publishing, Inc.
www.SirenPublishing.com

CPSIA information can be obtained at www.ICGtesting.com
Printed in the USA
BVOW08s1816100315

391096BV00008B/69/P